Mickey Cuffaro

What if you were given a ticket
that could magically start your life anew?
Would you redeem it?

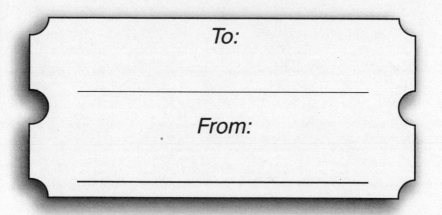

To:

_____

From:

_____

Please accept this invitation to discover for yourself
the greatest gift of all—life's golden ticket.

"Whatever you do, pay the price of admission for *Life's Golden Ticket*! This book is entertaining, provocative, and loaded with wisdom. Honestly, this is the most original book I've read in years."

 —**Bill Treasurer,** CEO, Giant Leap Consulting and
  author of *Right Risk: Ten Powerful Principles*
  for Taking Giant Leaps with Your Life

"Here is your 'golden ticket' to a terrific life. Read, absorb, and apply the wisdom in this story to rediscover and reclaim the life you were destined to live."

 —**Mark Victor Hansen,** co-creator, #1 *New York Times*
  bestselling series *Chicken Soup for the Soul,*® and
  co-author *Cracking the Millionaire Code* and *The*
  One Minute Millionaire

"Burchard brings impressive wisdom and simplicity to the complex task of changing our lives. The story is captivating and you will be able to apply and connect all of the concepts to your own personal challenges. Fantastic!"

 —**Rebecca Frechette,** national category manager,
  Target Stores

"This is a wonderful, warm, fast-moving parable of struggle and happiness that you will enjoy over and over again."

 —**Brian Tracy,** author of *The Psychology of*
  Achievement and *Goals!*

"Brendon Burchard writes a thought-provoking story that feels surprisingly personal and universally applicable at the same time. *Life's Golden Ticket* is a story you will want to share with those in your life—I did and ended up with three generations of fans!"

 —**Teri Babcock,** partner, Accenture

"*Life's Golden Ticket* is both engaging and inspiring. This book allows you to recognize that you can significantly improve the quality of your life—today."
—**Ralph L. Keeney,** co-author of *Smart Choices: A Practical Guide to Making Better Life Decisions*

"*Life's Golden Ticket* is wise without being preachy, inspiring without forgetting insight, entertaining without sacrificing empowerment. Brendon Burchard shows incredible depth, compassion, and wisdom on every page. He has given us a true gift."
—**Kelley Graham,** vice president, Levi Strauss & Company

"In these pages you will see yourself on your worst days and on your best. With Burchard's compassionate story as your guide, you will now understand the forces at work in both cases and learn to master them as never before."
—**Tim Ogilvie,** CEO, Peer Insight, LLC

"I read the story in one sitting—I just couldn't put it down. I cried, I laughed, I cheered, I wondered where it was all going—and when I finished, I was so thankful for the journey. The story convinces you that change is possible and the main character's journey shows you step-by-step how to achieve it. Something magical happens to you between the first page and the last. I'll never look at life the same way."
—**KC George,** corporate program manager, Visa USA

LIFE'S GOLDEN TICKET

LIFE'S GOLDEN TICKET

An Inspirational Novel

BRENDON BURCHARD

Doubleday Large Print
Home Library Edition

HarperSanFrancisco
A Division of HarperCollins*Publishers*

This Large Print Edition, prepared especially for Double-day Large Print Home Library, contains the complete, unabridged text of the original Publisher's Edition.

 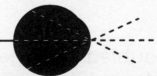
ISBN: 978-0-7394-8564-4

**This Large Print Book carries the
Seal of Approval of N.A.V.H.**

Dedicated to my parents,
Mel and Christiane Burchard,

and my brothers and sister,
David, Bryan, and Helen,
for surrounding me with the
beauty of faith, love, and friendship.
I am forever grateful. I love you all.

And to Denise.
Thank you, Sunshine,
for your support, patience, and belief in me.
I love you.

PROLOGUE

**Death twitches my ear. "Live," he says,
"I am coming."**
—Virgil

Ten years ago, while visiting a developing country, I survived a dramatic car accident. To this day I vividly recall the moment I physically pulled myself free from the twisted wreckage—because that was also the moment I emerged from the emotional depression that had recently made a wreck of my life.

The accident was a perfect metaphor for my life at that point: a journey down a dark road, a sharp turn, utter loss of control. In the previous few months I had been through a knockdown, drag-out catastrophe of a breakup with the first woman I ever loved. In that time I went from being a fairly happy, confident, outgoing kind of guy to a depressed, self-doubting recluse who pushed everyone away for fear of being hurt again. I seemed to have lost all control over my life. My thoughts became contaminated with self-loathing and, occasionally, suicidal messages.

In many ways, I suppose that my life was a wreck long before the night we took that sharp corner at eighty-five miles per hour.

Then everything changed in an instant. The road yawed out of view, replaced by a black void in the windshield as our car careened off the highway. The music on the radio died away, and the wind no longer whipped through the windows. All went silent for a moment as the car arced upward into the air, and I felt a sense of flight, of weightlessness. I thought, *Please, God, I'm not ready....*

When I awoke, I saw nothing but the car's headlights illuminating a darkened field of sugarcane through a narrow opening in front of me—an opening that was once the windshield. The dashboard and doors had been crushed inward, trapping the driver and me inside a tight compartment of warped metal and shattered glass and plastic. We struggled for what felt like hours to escape that coffinlike confinement.

I remember pulling myself through the windshield, standing on the crumpled hood of the car, looking down at my bloodied body, then up to the heavens. And that was the moment when everything changed. I suddenly felt lifted from the emotional wreckage that had been my life. All the hurt and anger and disgust and regret that had seethed in my body over the past few months were gone; the fog of doubt and despair had cleared. Ironically, instead of causing me pain, the accident had released me from it. A blissful flood of peace and gratitude swept through my body. I felt *free,* as if the gates to possibility had just opened before me for the first time in my life. It was as if I had been handed an invitation to start anew, to experience the world through new eyes and new senses—a world more abundant, colorful, and awe-inspiring than I could ever have imagined. It was as if, at that precise moment, I had been given a "golden ticket"—a second chance at life. After staring gratefully at the heavens for what seemed an eternity, I let out a deep sigh and felt *life* breathe back into me. For the first time in months, my soul sang.

**Here is the test to find whether
your mission on Earth
is finished: If you're alive, it isn't.**
—RICHARD BACH

Miraculously, the driver of the vehicle and I walked away from the accident with relatively few injuries. But the wreck's lesson stayed with me forever: you are lucky to be alive, you were left here for a reason, you can start anew any time you choose, now get busy— the clock is ticking.

Within a year of receiving my golden ticket, I was able to turn my life around. I found my confidence again. I worked on creating healthier, more beautiful relationships. I let a sense of freedom and faith guide me, and I began seeking significance more than success. By the first anniversary of my accident, I felt like I had a life that was truly my own— one that was directed by choice rather than chance.

Since then I've been striving to keep a promise I made the very moment I was handed my golden ticket. Standing alive atop that crumpled hood, I softly spoke these words, which I will never forget: *Oh, God,* I whispered, *thank you—thank you for the second chance. I promise I'll earn it.*

In order to earn my second shot at life, some part of me has always known that I had to take my golden ticket and share it with others. So I've spent the past decade trying to help other people come to that moment I reached so long ago: a moment when they sense the gates to possibility swinging open for them; a moment when they feel truly alive and free; a blessed moment when they feel as if they could start over again and create the life they have always wanted. This is the moment I invite you to experience by reading this book.

There will be a time when you believe everything is finished.
That will be the beginning.
—Louis L'Amour

When you have finished reading, I also invite you to share your moments of discovery with those you care about so that they may have similar experiences. Sometimes we can change the lives of those around us simply by sharing with them our own stories of trans-formation. Surely, life's golden ticket, with all its secrets, has always been handed down this way—person by person, story by story.

What exactly is life's golden ticket, and what kind of life does it gain us admission to? I believe you will find your own answers in the story ahead.

PART 1

PART 1

1
THE ENVELOPE

I was standing in the bathroom shaving when I heard the voice from the television: "We interrupt this program to report breaking news on the Mary Higgins disappearance."

I dropped the razor in the sink, threw a towel around my waist, and bolted for the living room. Mary's picture filled the left half of the screen. The stoic local evening news anchor said, "Miss Higgins, who mysteriously disappeared forty days ago, has reportedly been found. . . ."

Oh my God. I waited for the worst.

". . . A spokesperson for the Highway Patrol said Higgins was taken . . ."

The telephone rang, and I scrambled for it, still keeping an eye on the TV.

" . . . hospital just fifteen minutes ago, where she is reportedly . . ."

I snatched the phone in mid-ring. It was Mary's mother, Linda, talking so quickly I could catch only half of what she said.

"Linda, slow down," I said. "What's going on?"

" . . . We're here with her . . . you've got to get down here . . . they found her. . . . They *found Mary!*"

I glanced at the picture of Mary on the screen. "Jesus, Linda," I breathed. "It's on the news. Is she okay?"

"We're at the hospital. You've got to get down here . . . now!" she said.

"Linda, *is Mary okay?*"

"Just come over as fast as you can. Room four-ten. I gotta go. *Hurry.*"

The line went dead.

I burst into the hospital lobby and was blinded by camera flashes. A wall of reporters surrounded me, shoving their cameras and microphones in my face, barking questions.

"What is Mary's condition?" . . . "Do you know what happened?" . . . "Have you spoken with her parents?"

I'd never been so glad to see a nurse in my life. A sturdy woman in white pushed through the reporters and grabbed my forearm. "Give the man some privacy!" she commanded. "You—out of the way." She pulled me forward, parting the reporters with a running back's stiff-arm. Guiding me to the elevators, she shoved me in one and turned, blocking off the reporters behind her. "Fourth floor," she mouthed.

I pushed the button and felt a chill of dread at seeing the words next to it: INTENSIVE CARE.

The doors closed, muffling the reporters' shouted questions. I breathed in the sterile bleach-and-ether hospital smell, thinking how much I hated these places. Images of my grandfather, then my mother, flashed in my mind. *Please don't let it be like that,* I thought.

The doors opened. A nurse was at the desk.

"Ma'am, I'm looking for room four-ten. I'm—"

"I know," she said. "Go down the hall and take your first right. Fifth door on your left."

By the time she had said it I was halfway down the hall.

Rounding the corner, I saw Mary's mother, Linda, crying in her husband Jim's arms. A doctor was speaking to them quietly. A respectful distance away, Detective Kershaw, the officer in charge of the missing persons unit, stood staring at his feet.

I took a deep breath and tried to slow my heart. As I walked toward them I told myself to be strong.

Jim saw me first and whispered in Linda's ear. She wiped her tears, pulled away, and looked at me with sorrow-filled eyes.

Oh, no, I thought. *Please don't. . . .*

My face felt numb as I reached them.

"Linda, is she alive?"

Kershaw sat across from me, fidgeting with his notepad and glancing up every so often at one of those awful seaside paintings that seem to be the required decor on waiting room walls. He probably knew that if he looked me in the eye I'd take a swing at him. In a contrite voice, he said, "Look, I got you all wrong—I admit that. Finding Mary the way we did, it proves you had nothing to do with her disappearance."

"It's about time you figured that out, you—"

"Whoa, now," Kershaw said, leaning back and putting his hands in the air, palms out. "I know you're upset. But like I said, I was just doing my job. You can't blame me for thinking you had something to do with it. . . ."

Still seething, I said nothing.

"Okay," he said. "Look—I don't blame you. Let's just start over. Let's talk like two people who want to figure out how Mary ended up on that highway. I know we've been through this a thousand times, but can you tell me once more about the last time you saw her? Can you tell me exactly what she said again? Now that we know where she ended up, maybe there's a clue in your last conversation."

Our last "conversation," I'm sad to say, was a shouting match. Shame and regret flooded my heart when I thought about it.

We were screaming at each other in the kitchen. Mary was on another of her we've-got-to-change-our-lives rants. The same old fight—every night, it seemed, right after dinner, for the past six months. She was tired of me sitting in front of the TV after work, tired of my being "distant," tired of my cynicism, tired of feeling weak, tired of living a life that she considered below us. Tired, she said, of being tired.

"We're drowning here," she said. "Drowning in despair, in our own pools of pessimism." That was her favorite phrase in combat: "pools of pessimism."

"You don't know how lucky we have it," I shot back. "My folks would have *killed* for a pool."

A line like that usually broke her stride and cooled her down—I was always good at making her laugh and changing the subject. But not this time. Her face sagged, and she started to cry. After a few moments of sobbing, she looked up and said, "I think I need to go away for the weekend. . . . I was going to ask you to come with me, but I don't think you're ready."

She'd never said anything in a voice that serious before.

"Where are you going?" I asked. "I'm not ready for *what?*"

She paused. "Change—you're not ready for change."

Here we go again, I thought. I braced for the laundry list she'd been working the past two months: Get off the couch. Put the beer down. Quit moping. Open up. Tell me what's going on. That was Mary, always trying to control me, make me follow her rules for how to live, make me someone I was not—a bright, shiny, sensitive sap.

"Will you stop trying to *control* me all the time? I don't need another mother, and I don't need you to tell me how much I need to change. Just let me live my life."

"But you're *not* living your life," she cried. "You're hiding from it. You sit in front of that television every night, trying to forget the fact that your life is miserable."

There—she'd said it. I looked at her, shocked.

She looked down, her long eyelashes almost resting on her cheeks, and let out a sigh of exhaustion. "Like I said, you're not ready to change. But I am. And I'm going. A friend invited me to a place that can supposedly change my life. He said it's a place of magic that will challenge and inspire me, a place where my dreams could come true."

"Wow, honey, cool, you're going to Disneyland?"

"I'm serious. I'm going."

I laughed at her, not believing she would leave. "Say hi to Mickey for me," I said.

Her eyes widened, and she threw her coffee cup into the sink, where it shattered. She swiped her keys off the counter and headed for the door, saying, "I've heard this place can work miracles. For my sanity and for our relationship's sake, you'd better hope so."

She slammed the door behind her. I almost said, "Don't let the door hit you on the way out." But I hadn't, thank God.

That was forty days ago.

I never told Kershaw all the details of the fight—he didn't need to know. Besides, I trusted authority about as much as I trusted used-car salesmen. I knew he'd crucify me if he found out we were fighting when she left.

"You're right," I said to Kershaw as I stood up. "We *have* been through this a thousand times, and I've got nothing more to say to you." I turned to walk over to Mary's father, Jim, who was down the hall at the coffee machine.

"Okay," Kershaw said. "I'm sure we'll find out what happened to Mary when she . . . if she wakes up."

Jim had a cup of machine instant coffee ready for me.

"Here ya go," he said softly. He wasn't the kind of guy to cry, but his eyes looked red.

I looked at him, knowing I was to blame for this—all of it.

"Jim . . . I'm so sorry. . . ."

He raised his hand, cutting me off.

"Don't," he said gently. "It's not your fault. Forget Kershaw and all this mess in the media the last few weeks. There's nothing you could have done. You've got to tell yourself that. Linda and I believe that. We do. No matter what happened between you and Mary, we know it's not your fault she disappeared. And it's not your fault she's in here."

His voice cracked, and he looked toward Mary's room.

"I just find myself praying and wishing our little Mary could open her eyes and tell us what's been going on these past forty days. I just wish she could . . . tell us she's okay."

Tears streamed down his broad, strong face.

———

I felt my shoulder being nudged, and opened my eyes. Mary's doctor knelt in front of me.

"I must've fallen asleep," I said groggily.

"It's okay," he said. "But Mary is conscious, and I don't know how long she'll be that way. She's very fragile, and we don't know if she'll . . ." He shook his head. "She's asked for you."

I tried to jump to my feet, forgetting that I was lying across four waiting room chairs. I crashed to the floor, bruising my tailbone.

The doctor helped me to my feet and said, "Take it easy now. We'd rather have you as a visitor than a patient."

I shook the sleep from my head and sprinted down the hall to 410.

Linda was coming out. She gently closed the door behind her.

"She's conscious?" I asked, breathing hard.

"Yes," Linda said. "She can talk, but she's very weak and not making much sense. She keeps muttering something about a miracle. And she's asking for you." Linda was pale, and the fine lines on her face looked deeper. "Talk to her. . . . Tell her you love her. It might be the last . . ." She paused in the doorway, smiling sadly. "Just tell her you love her."

It was dark except for a dim light over Mary's head. I'd been in the room several times in the past few hours, but still I had to fight back the tears when I saw her lying there. Her head was swathed in bandages, and her cheeks looked fat, pushed up by the collar of a neck brace. Her right leg was elevated, frozen in place in a thick cast. A half-dozen machines sighed and beeped around her in a terrifying, tuneless chorus; her breath came in short, painful rasps. Every inch of her soft skin seemed to be bruised and bloated.

I just couldn't understand it. She had been standing on an old roadway up in the mountains when the truck hit her. What was she doing out there?

"Honey," I whispered, leaning over the bed rail. "Honey, it's me. . . ."

Nothing.

I brushed her cheek. "Honey, *please*. . . ." I choked back a sob. "I'm so sorry."

She opened her eyes.

"Hey, you," she said through cracked lips. "It's okay." Her voice was so delicate I could barely hear.

The words gushed out in a torrent. "Mary, I'm so sorry. I love you so much. I'm so sorry. I'm so sorry, honey."

Her lips crooked up into half a smile; her quick, alert gaze surprised me.

"Everything's going to be okay," she said tenderly. As if *I* were the one lying in bed, about to die.

"Mary, you've been in an accident. You're in the hosp—"

"I know. It's okay."

I looked at her with wonder.

She spoke softly and slowly. "I have something to tell you. . . . I have to ask you to do something for me."

"Anything," I said, trying desperately to keep the tears at bay. "Anything."

She drew a deep breath. "Bowman's Park. I need you to go back there for me. For *you*."

I shook my head. Bowman's Park?

Her eyes fixed on mine. "Yes, Bowman's. You need to go there."

My mind reeled. Bowman's was an old amusement park up in the mountains. They shut it down twenty years ago after a small boy—Mary's eight-year-old brother—fell to his death from the Ferris wheel.

A few years after the park closed, rumors had floated that it was haunted. The rumors rose and subsided every few years with the incoming freshman classes at the local high schools. A year and a half ago, though, the allegations took a strange twist, and suddenly the place went from haunted to holy. A bunch of crazies started saying that miracles were happening up there. The local news stations scrambled to investigate but, of course, turned up nothing. No one who claimed to have witnessed any miracles would talk about them.

"Mary," I said softly, still shaking my head, "you weren't at Bowman's Park. I know that's where your brother died, but it's closed, remember? You were miles from there, all the way on the other side of the mountain."

"I know. . . . Listen," she said, the strength in her voice waning. "I *was* there. And now *you* have to go, or you won't understand. Find my coat. There's an envelope in the pocket. *Don't open it.* Take it to the park gate. Give the envelope to my brother."

Tears stung my eyes. She was obviously delirious. She even thought her brother was alive. How could our last conversation on earth go like this? The doctor had warned me that she was heavily sedated, likely to be drifting between reality and dreams, but this was madness. I turned so she didn't have to see me cry.

"Wait," she said, straining. "Look at me."

I turned back, tears flowing freely now.

She took another long breath. "You remember the rumors? About miracles at the park?"

"Yes."

"That's why I went there—we needed a miracle. . . ."

How could I have let it get so bad between us that she was reduced to grasping at such straws?

Her eyes widened. "The rumors are true."

She paused. Her face strained, and her eyes blinked. I worried that she might pass out. "Miracles . . ." she repeated. "Get the envelope . . . go . . . find out what happened to me . . . experience what I did . . . Go. . . ."

Her slender fingers grasped my arm with as much strength as she could muster, which wasn't much. "Promise me you'll go there . . . *right now.*"

"Mary," I cried, hot tears running down my face, my chest constricting in pain. "Honey, I'm not leaving you."

She gave a soft cry, as though something hurt her deep inside. Her hand fell back to the bed. "If you don't go now . . . you'll never know what happened. . . ."

She paused, closing her eyes tight. "Promise me you'll go—the second you walk out of this room."

I shook my head. "I won't leave you."

Her body tensed; her breath came in shallow pants. "Go . . . *now!*"

I stood silently stroking her hand, not knowing what to say. My tears splashed silently off the thin hospital blanket. A tear struck her hand, and her brow wrinkled. She took a long breath in and pushed out a soft whimper: "*Promise,*" she whispered, her lips quivering and her voice trailing away.

That was it then; I had no choice—this was her last wish. I closed my eyes and tried to think of what to say before she was gone.

"I promise," I said softly. Still holding her hand, I leaned in and kissed her forehead. My voice cracked. "I'll love you forever."

Her lips curved into a faint smile as she mouthed, "I love you."

Then her eyes closed, and the tension left her face.

The bank of machines around her beeped and whirred loudly.

What do you mean, you're leaving?" Linda looked at me in disbelief. "Now?"

"Yes," I said sheepishly. I didn't know how to explain what Mary had said, or what I had promised her I would do.

A nurse had given me Mary's jacket—it was crusted with blood. Linda and Jim looked at it fearfully as I fidgeted with it.

"Are you sure you should be going anywhere right now?" Jim asked, giving me a look of concern.

"I, uh . . . I made a promise to Mary. I have to do something for her right now. I'll be back in a few hours. I know it's crazy, but I gave her my word. I've got to go." I couldn't tell them where I was going. How could I tell them I was going to Bowman's Park, where their first child had died?

Linda's mouth parted slightly to speak, but neither of them said anything. I kept wringing Mary's jacket in my hands.

After an awkward moment, Jim said, "Okay, son. If Mary wanted you to do something, go do it."

Linda looked surprised. She looked at Jim, then back at me. Shaking her head, she said, "I don't understand. I mean, right now? I just don't see . . ."

Jim turned quickly, hugging her. He looked back at me. "Do what you have to do," he said. "We'll handle things here. We'll see you at the house?"

I nodded, then embraced each of them.

As I opened the exit stairway door, I heard Linda crying, asking God why all of this had happened.

I wanted to go back and explain. But then, I didn't understand either.

I sneaked out the back of the hospital to avoid the news cameras.

2
ADMISSION CHARGES

The pickup jolted as I pulled off the highway and onto the gravel road leading to the park. The white, dollar-sized envelope from Mary's jacket slid along the dash as I wheeled around a curve. The crinkled paper was blotched red with drops of her blood.

A cloud of dust billowed in my rearview mirror. I drove fast, anticipation making my foot heavy. The sun was sinking in the sky, and I wanted to get in and out of the park before nightfall. I had been thinking on the trip up—maybe I should visit the old Ferris wheel where Todd was killed and bury the envelope there. She wanted him to have it.

As I approached the park, I drove under a thick canopy of pine branches that hung above the road, blocking the last rays of sun. The narrow lane, pocked with potholes and littered with dead branches, looked as though no one had traveled it since the flurry of news features had caused all the speculation a year and a half ago. Before that, almost no one had come out here since Todd's death, nearly twenty years ago.

I pounded over the rutted road for four more miles until I reached the broad clearing at the end. Squinting through the dusty windshield, I saw an enormous, overgrown field of grass bordered by pine trees. A few hundred yards away, the entrance archway still stood. A rotting fence ran from the pillars supporting the archway all the way out to the woods bordering the field. From the archway hung a laminated wood sign: BOWMAN'S PARK.

Beyond the entrance stood six dilapidated ticket booths, a listing flagpole, some rickety park benches, and, a hundred yards farther in, the circular skeleton of the old Ferris wheel. I remembered that soon after Todd's accident the Bowman company went bust and wasn't even able to clean up the site. I also remembered Jim once telling me he had requested that the Ferris wheel be left standing as a memorial. Bowman obliged, though they removed the carriage seats so that no one would get hurt climbing on them after the park closed.

I eased my foot off the brake, letting the pickup roll softly onto the field of grass and out from under the canopy of pine and fir. The fading sun warmed the left side of my face, and I turned toward it. Then I froze at the sight, about fifty yards away, of Mary's car.

I parked next to the Honda and got out. The mountain air was crisp, and the sounds of birds and insects filled my ears. I got out and tried her car door—locked. Odd. Maybe she had locked herself out and tried to walk home.

I grabbed her jacket from the truck and went through the pockets. Her keys were there. Maybe her car wouldn't start.

I unlocked the Honda, slid into the driver's seat, and put the keys in the ignition. It started right up.

Why had she left her car here? How had she ended up on the other side of the mountain?

As I got out of her car, the birds stopped singing. It was quiet for a moment—unnaturally so. Then the sounds of children and laughter filled the air.

I scrambled out of the car in surprise and peered back toward where I had entered the field.

Four little boys played tag just in front of the archway leading into the park.

I looked for other cars in the clearing. Nothing.

"Hey!" I shouted. "Kids! Hey! Where are your parents?"

They kept playing as though they had never heard me.

I ran around to the truck cab, threw Mary's jacket inside, grabbed the envelope from the dash, and shoved it into my back pocket. I trotted to the archway. The kids didn't seem to notice my approach.

"Hey!" I said again as I neared them. "Where are your folks?"

One of the boys looked at me and smiled. Then he and the others ran through the arch and vanished.

I stopped dead.

The boys' laughter echoed.

I spun around, scanning the field. I was alone. I stood in surprised silence for a few moments.

"Hello? *Hello-o?* Anybody around?"

No reply.

I took a few steps toward the archway, looking up at it as if it were going to tell me where the boys had gone. Two steps. Three. Four. I stepped under the archway and was hit by a cacophony of sound: kids laughing, rides whirring, cars honking, barkers shouting.

I shook my head, squeezing my eyes shut. When I opened them, I couldn't believe it. All around me were hundreds of people, surging and streaming into six lines, one for each ticket booth. The booths looked freshly painted. Past the booths and rising above them, the Ferris wheel spun, lights twinkling brightly. Large red-and-white-striped tents flapped softly in the evening breeze. Clowns walked this way and that, selling cotton candy and balloons. A Loop-de-Loop rattled in the distance, its riders screaming with glee. Barkers hollered to young men, encouraging them to win a stuffed bear "for the little lady." "Step right up, folks, to the greatest game on the planet!"

This couldn't be.

I shook my head in disbelief, but nothing changed. Turning about, I was met with another inconceivable sight: the parking lot was full of cars, parking, pulling out, honking, waiting. The entire empty, overgrown field was packed. I strained to see my truck. It was still there, next to Mary's car, in a row of thirty or more vehicles.

I staggered backward, awestruck. Several people walked past, looking at me with concern—as if *I* were the one out of place. I took a few more steps back and tripped on something. I crashed to the ground, landing on my tailbone for the second time in a matter of hours. A knifing pain shot up my back.

"Hey, mister, are you okay?"

I looked up to see an elderly man with a long, kind face. He wore faded blue zip-up coveralls and beaten brown work boots. He leaned on a broom.

"I didn't see you there. I'm sorry, son. Let me help you up." He extended a hand and pulled me to my feet.

He asked again, "You okay?"

I couldn't speak. My tongue was trapped in a mouth stunned with surprise. The groundskeeper looked a little like my grandfather, only older. Grandpa had passed away when I was twelve. He was seventy-six when he died.

"I . . . uh . . . I'm sorry I kicked your broom, sir," I mumbled. "Are you . . . do I know you?"

"Don't think so. Name's Henry," he said, drawing his left forefinger across the name patch on his coveralls. He smiled at me and bent down to pick up a dustpan and a small garbage bag. "Oh, and don't worry about the broom—people are always in a hurry to get inside. I'm used to getting bumped."

Then he turned and, with an arcing swoop of the broom, called back, "You have yourself a good time, sonny."

I watched him go back to sweeping, then cried out, "Wait—Henry!" I was immediately embarrassed by the desperate tone in my voice.

Henry turned back with a puzzled look.

I took a few steps toward him. "So, uh, you say everyone's always in a hurry. You . . . work here long?"

A smile stretched across his face. "Oh, long enough, I suppose." He held up his callused hands.

I continued to stumble along. "Is this place . . . uh . . . is it . . . are you for *real*?"

Henry laughed heartily. "Ha! For real! Well, tell you what, the missus used to tell her friends I was too good to be true, but she'd always tell me something different when the dishes weren't done!" He slapped the leg of his coveralls with delight.

I smiled politely, so confused and stunned that I couldn't feel anything resembling a laugh anywhere within me.

Henry picked up on my confusion. "Now, why the long face? We all want a return to the summers of our childhood, don't we? Here's your chance," he said, waving toward the park. His voice was deep, rhythmic, and warm.

I glanced at the smiling faces of people passing by. "I'm afraid I'm not here for fun, Henry. I'm here to find out what happened to my fiancée."

"Oh," Henry said. "What do you mean?"

"Well, she was here. Her car's parked outside. But something happened. She was in an accident. She's in the hospital. She made me promise to come here. She told me to find out what she experienced, and give her brother an envelope."

Henry's brow furrowed with compassion. "An accident? What happened?"

"I don't know. All I know is, she must have been here. She ended up on the other side of that mountain," I said, gesturing at the wooded mountain rising behind the park. "She wound up on a highway road over there, and she was . . . she was hit by a truck." I paused, and my eyes started to burn with tears. "Anyway, she made me promise to come here."

Henry seemed genuinely saddened. He said softly, "I'm so sorry." He looked to the ground, as if searching for the right words, and then shot me a look of confusion. "I just realized what you said a second ago. Let me understand something, son. Are you saying you *don't know* what she experienced here?"

"No, I don't understand. She just told me to take an envelope from her jacket, come here, find out what happened to her, and deliver the envelope to her brother."

Henry looked at me intently. "What was your fiancée's name?"

"Mary. Mary Higgins."

"Do you have the envelope on you now?" Henry asked, holding his gaze on me tightly.

"Uh, yeah. I do."

He held out his hand. "Can I see it?"

It seemed an odd request, but I pulled the envelope from my hip pocket and offered it to him.

Henry took it and said, "Oh, my. She never opened it."

His words unnerved me. "What?"

"Something went wrong," he said uneasily.

My mind raced. "What went wrong? Do you know Mary? Did you see her here? What happened to her?" As I blurted the questions, Henry didn't take his eyes off the envelope.

"Hold on," he said, "let me think."

A painful minute of anticipation went by.

"You were engaged to Mary?" Henry asked.

"Yes. *Do you know her?*"

"I do not," he said flatly. "I don't know Mary, and I don't know exactly what happened to her. Everyone comes here for different purposes, and everyone experiences something different. But I do know something went wrong. If she never opened this envelope," he said, turning it over in his hands, "then something inside the park went badly wrong." He looked at me and shook his head, as if deciding something. "I'm going to help you find out what happened," he said. "There's just one problem."

"What?"

Henry stared at the ticket booths and asked, "You don't have an invitation to get in, do you?"

The sky's amber hues faded into the heavier colors of dusk. The lights of the park blinked on, and each soon had a squadron of moths orbiting it. A faint strip of blue still bordered the tree-lined horizon. The night brought a pleasant coolness to the air. I stood behind Henry in the ticket line, hoping his plan would work.

"Just remember," he said as the woman in front of us walked to the booth window, "you can't get in here on your own. So keep quiet once I start talkin'."

The woman in front of us passed something through a hole in the ticket booth. I couldn't see the booth attendant, but the woman smiled at the person inside. Then she walked through the metal turnstile that separated us from the inside of the park.

"Next, please!" a booming female voice called out from the ticket booth.

Admission Charges

Henry motioned me forward. I stepped up to the window and, on seeing its occupant, stopped immediately. She was massive, occupying almost the entire booth. Her jaw was working on a hot dog, and her left hand held a gigantic Slurpee. Ketchup and mustard leaked out of the hot dog, staining her tent-like yellow sundress. The window of the booth was clouded with steam. A small fan blew inside, but beads of sweat still formed on her wide brow. She grunted as she shoved more of the hot dog into her mouth.

"What can I do for you, kid?" she said around the mouthful of hot dog.

I couldn't remember the last time I had been called "kid." I continued to gawk until Henry gave me a gentle nudge in the ribs.

"Oh. Hi. Uh, I'm here to enter the park."

"That's novel," she said sarcastically, more interested in her Slurpee than in me. "Where's your invitation?"

Henry gave me another elbow, this time to move me out of the way. He centered himself in front of the glass. "Betty, my dear, how are we today?"

Betty stopped chewing at the sound of his voice. "Henry? What are *you* doing here?"

She put the hot dog down and tried to wipe the condiments from her mouth and dress. By her tone, I got the impression Henry had some pull at the park.

Henry slid Mary's envelope to Betty and waited for her to examine it. He also positioned his body so I was out of her view. Standing to the side of the booth, I couldn't see Betty's face anymore, just her puffy white hands as they turned the envelope over.

"This is serious, Henry," she said.

Henry stared at her intently.

"I bet you want to get to the bottom of this," she said, her voice dropping to a deeper tone. "But you know the consequences of sponsoring this kid. Are you sure you're ready? Are you sure he's the right one?"

Henry nodded slowly.

A long moment passed, and Betty leaned forward, peering at me.

"Okay, kid. Big Betty will go easy on you today, even if you are a little ugly."

She burst out laughing at her joke, rattling the entire booth. Then she struggled to turn her bulk, to snatch a paper form from a bin above her right shoulder.

"Read this," she said. "Sign it. That's it."

She pushed the form through the window. Her hands were twice the size of mine.

The form was a simple piece of paper entitled "PRICE OF ADMISSION." The form had four check boxes down the left side, with a statement next to each one. At the bottom was a line for my signature. The statements read:

☐ I agree to give up my dependency on my present experience and be open to possibility.

☐ I agree to give up my defense mechanisms and face the truth.

☐ I agree to give up my belief that change equals pain.

☐ I agree to give up my impulses to quit or leave my host's side.

What kind of amusement park made you sign a contract to get in?

I read the statements and looked at Henry. "This is it?"

"That's it," he said. "Take it seriously."

Betty added, "You don't know how lucky you are to have met Henry, kid."

Henry nodded for me to sign. Once I did, I slid it back to Betty. She picked up a rubber stamp, but hesitated before touching the paper.

"Henry," I heard her whisper, "you *really* sure about this one?"

Henry leaned in and said something inaudible.

She looked once more in my direction, her eyes narrowing, then stamped the form and slid Mary's envelope back to the caretaker. He handed it to me, and I put it back in my hip pocket.

"Kid," she said to me, "you're in. You're the last one today, I guess." She pointed behind me; strangely, there wasn't a soul in sight. I looked into the park and saw an open square with a flagpole in the center. There were no people there either.

"You be good to Henry," Betty commanded. "We love him here, and he just vouched for you, so be thankful. Now get going."

With considerable effort, Betty stood up. She bumped up against the walls as she turned to leave her post.

As Henry gestured for me to follow him through the turnstiles, I glanced back at the booth to see Betty huffing and squirming to reach for the door.

Henry and I entered the park, and just a few feet inside we were stopped by a loud crashing. I turned around to see the door of Betty's ticket booth swing open and a little girl jump out.

She couldn't have been more than eight. She wore a cute, bright yellow sundress. Smiling, she skipped into the open square and disappeared behind one of the red-and-white-striped tents.

I looked back at the booth, openmouthed.

Empty.

I turned to Henry. "Did she just . . . did you . . . did I just see . . . ?"

Henry waited patiently for me to find my words.

"Did I just . . . see what I think I saw?"

He touched my shoulder softly and smiled. "Maybe it's time I told you what goes on here in the park."

3
THE TRUTH BOOTH

The open square just inside the park was about eighty feet on a side. A soft breeze slapped the lanyard against the hollow pole. The walls of the tents that bordered the square moved gently in the breeze. Other than that, the square was eerily silent—no more shuffling, jostling people, calling barkers, or spinning Ferris wheel.

"What is this place, Henry?"

Henry looked around the square thoughtfully. "*That* I can't quite explain. It's where miracles happen. It's a place where people become what they've always dreamed of being. I s'pose that's why you saw Betty become a beautiful, happy, healthy little girl—so you could see this is a place where people can transform themselves."

"But how did it appear, how did this place just . . . ?"

Henry shook his head and interrupted. "No questions like that. Let's start with a simple ground rule. No questions about how the park came to be, or what it is, from here on out. If you question it, the experience isn't what it should be." He gave me a take-it-or-leave-it look. "Just accept that this could be a place of miracles for you, and choose to experience It fully. Got it?"

"Okay, but . . ."

"And no buts," he countered. "Now, come with me . . . ."

He walked to the far side of the square, and I could do nothing but follow obediently. I felt an urge to ask more questions, but I was so unsettled by the happenings of the past few hours that I couldn't even muster the logic to put the words together. Even if I could, Henry had already warned me.

When we got to the edge of the square, he said, "This is the Truth Booth." It was tiny, like one of those mini–photo booths kids and love-struck couples gravitate toward at shopping malls. "In a few minutes," he said, "I'm going to have you sit in there, and we're going to figure out some of the reasons you might be here. You see, everyone who comes to this park was invited by someone who cared deeply for them. And they accepted the invitation because they knew this place might just change their lives. That's why Mary would have come here: to change something. Most folks who get here, though, only have a vague notion of what they want to change. The Truth Booth helps them get clarity by forcing them to look at the reality of their lives. But before you go in there, you have some questions for me, don't you?"

He had read my mind. In the moments he had been talking, logic had returned, and I had fixed on the one question I couldn't leave alone.

"I'm sorry for asking again . . . but are you sure you don't know what happened to Mary?"

Henry studied me for a second, shaking his head. "I'm afraid I don't know *exactly* what happened to Mary. Everyone who comes here has a unique experience. They all go on rides, play games, eat, and walk around thinking about their lives, but exactly what they experience and what they learn differs for each individual. I can also say that everyone who comes here ends up confronting some things about their lives that may not be pleasant. Sometimes in that process people freak out, shut down, or get lost. I fear one of those things may have happened somewhere along the journey for Mary, but I just don't know. We'll have to figure it out together. But let me be clear about something," he said, positioning himself directly in front of me. "We are not here together simply to understand Mary's story. This is a place of destiny. There is a reason *you* are here—a reason beyond Mary, a reason you could even see this park without an invitation, a reason you bumped into me, and, somehow, a reason I felt deep down that I should help you. Everything happens for a reason."

"Why did you help?" I asked. "Betty made it sound like a big deal."

"It *is* a big deal," he said, offering no further explanation. "Look, son, Mary asked you to come here to understand what she experienced. Fine. But you are also here to understand something about yourself. There are lessons for you here. I'll be your guide—I believe I was meant to be. I've been here a very long time and have never heard of someone *not* opening their envelope at the end of their experience. There is unfinished business here. Our challenge in uncovering what happened to Mary is that this park works on *you* and no one else. So here's my advice: Don't try to understand what happened to Mary, because this experience will be more about you than about her. Trust that her story will unfold eventually along with your own, okay?"

I nodded but didn't really understand. I looked down, trying to sort it all out in my head. I felt helpless. I didn't know what to do, or think, or say. I felt frustrated: this was all too crazy—I just wanted to know what happened to Mary and then get out of there, wherever "there" was.

"It's called overwhelm," Henry said softly, picking up on my feelings. "You're going to be dealing with some pretty big issues, and you'll feel it more and more as we go. This experience, where you will be forced to change and learn and accept some tough truths about yourself will be unnerving. Like I said, you're just going to have to go along with this and figure it out piece by piece. And you're going to have to have faith that there is a reason for all this—a powerful reason why you are here. Now, let's get on with it."

He pulled back the Truth Booth's curtain and motioned for me to step inside. I climbed in, took a seat, and looked around. I was sitting in front of a television screen with two credit card–size slots beneath it.

As I stared at the blank screen, Henry said, "Get comfortable. This might not be easy. When I close the curtain, put your right hand on the screen in front of you. You'll figure it out from there." He gave me a last warm look from around the curtain. "You okay?"

I looked back, unsure. "I don't know. . . . This is all pretty wild. I just want to know what happened to Mary."

"I know. But think: Is it possible she wanted you to experience what she did? In fact, isn't that what you told me she said to you?"

"Yes, she said that."

"Okay," Henry said. "You're about to begin a similar experience. Yours will be unique to your life, but you'll get the idea. I'm going to close the curtain now, okay?"

"Um . . . all right."

He smiled in approval. "Now, just be honest, son. Be totally, completely honest. It will help."

He swept the curtain shut. It was pitch-black inside the booth. I reached forward and put my right hand on the tiny television screen, as Henry had told me. It quickly grew warm. Then it started to glow a light pink. Warmer. Then red. Warmer. Then purple. Hot! I pulled my hand away. The screen faded to black; then a small, gray, fuzzy image appeared. The image seemed far away. It started to come into focus ... closer.... It looked like the outline of someone's head ...closer.... It looked like a face ... closer ... clearer ...

I shot backward in surprise, slamming my head into the wall.

It was my mother's face in black-and-white. She looked exactly as she had the last time I saw her alive, when I was seventeen.

My mouth hung open. I leaned forward and touched the image of her face.

The image came alive. She spoke. "Hi, honey."

I pulled my hand away and slammed back into the wall again. My heart nearly leaped out of my chest. I could *hear* my pulse in the dark booth.

She was so real. She blinked, looking at me expectantly.

I shook my head. She couldn't be real. "Mom?"

"Don't be afraid," she said. "I'm here to ask you some questions. We don't have much time, and I love you, so let me begin straight-away. Are you happy?" Her voice sounded soothing and soft, as it always had. Her eyes were kind and engaged.

I shook my head in disbelief at what I was seeing. "Mom? It can't be you."

"It's me. But let's hurry. . . ."

"Mom, I . . ." I felt silly talking to the screen, but the words tumbled out anyway: "Mom, I miss you, I miss you so much. . . ."

Her face took on that knowing, patient look. "Don't cry, son. I miss you too. But please listen—we really don't have much time together. I have to ask you some questions. Tell me: are you happy?"

Through my tears, I saw a sense of urgency in her face.

"Yeah, Mom . . . I'm . . . I'm doing good. . . . You know you never need to worry about me."

She smiled and gave me her don't-even-try-to-fool-your-mother look. "That's what you used to tell me when you were a boy. You and I both knew it wasn't true then. You never wanted me to worry; you're a good son for that. But I need you to tell me the truth. Is your life going the way you expected? The way you dreamed?"

"Mom, why are you asking me these things? Why is this happening?"

"I can't tell you that. But you need to tell *me:* is your life what you dreamed it would be?"

I paused and looked away, not wanting to answer. *Besides, this isn't real . . . right?*

"Son?" she asked.

I looked back at her, and her kind eyes pulled a response from deep within me. "No, Mom. It's not what I dreamed of. . . . Life has taken some unexpected turns."

She nodded, brushing her dark, softly curling hair off her face. Smiling, she said, "Well, you were always good with directions. Where'd you get off track?"

"I don't know. . . . A lot of places, I guess."

"Where?"

"A lot of places. It's not that my life is bad. It's just . . . I know there's more."

"Let's pinpoint where there could be more. Work?"

"Maybe," I said.

"Maybe?" she said, arching her brow.

"Yes," I said.

Her eyes narrowed. "Yes maybe?"

"Okay. Definitely. I'm restless at work. . . . I could do better, something more me, something more fulfilling."

"There you go," she said. "If work is one of the unexpected turns you mentioned, then it's time to turn it around by admitting it. The truth is always a good turning point. What else isn't going well?"

I could hardly think how to tell her about Mary. I always wished they could have met.

"Are you in love?"

I looked at her in surprise. She seemed to read my mind. The thought of talking about Mary created a heavy lump in my throat.

"Yeah, Mom . . . a great lady. Her name's Mary."

"How's your relationship been with her?"

My eyes started to sting again. "Uh, well, you know, it's been—it was . . . a little rough." I didn't know how to tell her that I had pushed Mary away and that it was probably my fault she got into the accident.

"Has she been good to you?"

"Yes," I said, my voice trembling. "Always. She was always good to me. She was always patient, always trying to help me be better."

"Have you been good to her?"

The memory of screaming at Mary before she disappeared burned in my mind.

"Have you been good to her?" Mom asked again.

I doubled over in my seat and did my best to hold back tears. "I tried! I tried to be a good man. But I don't think I was."

A few moments passed, and I looked up to see Mom sobbing softly too.

"I'm sorry this is so hard. I know you always do your best."

I couldn't look at her. "Mom, I just don't know what to do anymore."

"Sure, you do. You always do, and you always did. Just be a good person, like you've always been." She paused until I looked back. "Listen, you were always a strong boy, a smart boy, a caring boy. Don't let what happened between you and your father convince you otherwise. Don't you dare settle for anything other than the life you want to live. Look at your life. Look at every area. See what you need to stop doing and what you need to start, and do it while you still can, no matter how hard it is. Do what your grandpa always told you: 'Just keep learning and living.'"

A minute passed as Mom waited for me to regain my composure.

"It's time for me to go now," she whispered.

"No, Mom! Not yet. . . . I have so many questions."

"I'm sorry, son, I've got to go. But let me say one last thing. You can be whoever you want to be, and you can do whatever you want to do. I always told you that, and I know you used to believe it. It's time to believe again, son. Promise me you'll keep that in mind?"

Tears flowed again as soon as she said the word *promise.* I had made two promises, to the two most important women in my life, in less than a day.

"I promise." I paused, floundering for words. "Mom, I wish you were really here," I said slowly. "I love you so much."

Her image started to fade. She smiled. "I'll always love you. . . ."

"Mom! No, don't go!"

" . . . Remember your promise. . . ."

"Mom! Don't go!"

The screen went blank.

Henry led me across the square without saying a word. The night was cooler than before but still comfortable. The faint hiss of the Victorian gaslights filled the air. When we arrived at a tent on the other side, he pulled back the entry flap and motioned for me to enter.

"What now?" I asked quietly, still choked up.

"Now we see the wizard."

4
THE STAGING TENT

I pushed through the tent flap and stopped in my tracks. The outside of the tent couldn't have been more than thirty feet by thirty. Inside, though, a different view made me blink in disbelief. I was standing at the top of an immense underground cavern.

I turned to Henry, and gasped.

He chuckled. "And you thought *Betty* was big."

The cavern opened out like a large concert hall. I looked down on what looked like a hundred rows of stadium-style seating, squinting to see the stage at the far end. The space was dimly lit, with hundreds of bare lightbulbs along the sidewalls. Limestone formations rose from the ground here and there and hung from the ceiling. The air was musty, but charged with excitement and the clamor of voices.

"Let's hurry up and go down front," Henry said and began descending the stairway.

How can this be possible? I turned around and pushed the tent flap back open. Cool air breezed in, and I saw that the lights illuminating the open square had been turned off. The stillness seemed dreamlike. I took a step outside to examine how a small tent could hold such a massive cavern.

"Believe me," Henry called from behind, "the show is in here."

He waved me toward him with a childlike smile. Dropping the flap, I started toward the stage. The stairs seemed larger than normal, and I felt like a kid climbing down boulders. The noise in the cavern grew with anticipation. I passed rows and rows of people. Many of them smiled at me as I worked my way down. Some talked excitedly with one another, while others just sat quietly, in awe at the grandeur of the space.

When we neared the bottom of the cavern, I turned around to see its true expansiveness. I whispered, "There must be *two thousand* people in here."

"It's something, isn't it?" Henry smiled broadly and gestured to me to sit in one of two open seats next to the aisle, about five rows back from the stage.

As I sat the lights suddenly turned off, and the crowd hushed.

Moments passed, and a soft blue spotlight beam illuminated a stool. I heard murmurs from the front and could just make out the dark outline of two people climbing the stairs at the right of the stage. A small girl and an old man wearing a hooded white cloak came into view as they neared the spotlight. The girl helped him forward, eased him onto the stool, pulled back his hood, and then ran offstage.

I shifted in my seat to get a better look. The old man looked like a stereotypical comic book wizard: long, flowing white hair and a long white beard. His cloak was tied in the middle with a simple gold-colored rope and fell over his feet. The wrinkles on his face said he was old; his hunched posture and inability to get to the stool on his own said he was *really* old.

He sat, eyes closed in silence. An entire minute passed, then another . . . and another. The crowd began to mumble. The blue spotlight gave him an eerie cast, as if he were cold and dead. Another minute. I turned to say something to Henry when the wizard raised one gaunt finger. The crowd fell silent again. Another minute.

Then he opened his startling blue eyes and sat straight up. His face grew animated, as if he had inhaled life itself.

"Friends," he said, drawing out the word, "welcome. Everything you have ever experienced in your life has served a purpose: it has brought you here, to this exact point. Your struggles and your survival and your tragedies and your triumphs brought you here. To this night. To this hour. To this moment." The wizard's rich, deep voice resonated throughout the cavern. The slight echo and the silent beginning brought a sense of importance and occasion to his words.

"You have come here because you received an invitation. You are all the same. You all surely felt your mother's embrace as a child. You all played with toys. All saw fireworks. Felt the nervousness of a first date. Heard the sting of criticism. Shrugged off conformity, then embodied it. Took a job. Sought love, gave love, lost love, sought it again. Grew stronger, wiser, more cynical. Cherished the glory days, bewailed the gloomy days, prayed for better days. And now you are here. And *I* am here to guide you through the next moments."

The wizard seemed to become younger with every word he spoke. His physical frailty was overshadowed by the power of his voice.

"Now, friends, to the question that was in your head when you arrived at this magical place, the question that echoed in your mind as you stood in line outside. The question that flashed across your eyes when you saw this cavern and sat on its cool stone, anticipating what might come next. The question of all humanity . . ."

" . . . Why . . . am . . . I . . . here?"

As he spoke the question, I felt myself release a breath that I hadn't even known I was holding. A collective sigh rose from the crowd.

The wizard's eyes sparkled as he heard recognition, and a lively grin stole over his face. "Oh, good. With all the buildup, I was hoping to get that right."

The crowd erupted into rolling laughter. The wizard practically glowed onstage.

"I have wandered this park for decades," he continued. "I know that everyone who has ever entered its gates has asked, '*Why have I come here?*' And after all this time I have come to realize that the answer to this question, like all great questions, lies in the question itself."

He paused and leaned so far forward that he looked as though he might fall off his stool. "Listen closely, for I am but a weak old wizard," he said, as if about to tell the greatest secret in the world.

I found myself leaning forward too.

"Friends," he said softly in a voice of occasion and finality, "you have *come* here so that you may *be*come." He drew in a breath and sat silently surveying the crowd's reaction to his words.

I replayed the line in my head: *You have* come *here so that you may* be*come.* Become what? The line felt a little anticlimactic. I looked to Henry for his reaction and found him still eyeing the wizard. I looked down the row and saw that most people were similarly enthralled—you could hear a pin drop.

The wizard wiggled back to the center of the stool. "I suspect that my answer, friends, has only brought you more questions. Maybe this is a good answer, then. It lets me speak a little longer before they put me back in the dungeon."

The crowd laughed once again.

He continued. "Now, the problem with my statement is that you can't help but ask the question: 'Become what?'"

I nodded.

"'Become *what?*' has become ingrained in your brains. You've been raised with the question '*What* should I *do* with my life?' That question, of course, is secondary. The primary question is, '*Who* should I *be* in my life?'

"You are here because you are restless over who you have *be*come. It is not your dissatisfaction with your job or what you *do* that has brought you to this park. It is not dissatisfaction with your family. Or your relationship. Or your finances. Or your neighborhood or your home or your car. It is a quiet dissatisfaction with *yourself,* with *who* you have become. You feel there is something *more* inside you, and you have come here searching for ways to dig it up and unleash it into the world. Deep down, you *know* you are more than what society has said you are or told you to be, and you are here to begin the great quest of proving it to the world and to yourself.

"I am here for one reason: to help you break a sinister spell that has held you in its thrall most of your adult lives. Yes, a spell. You have been hexed. You have been cursed. You have been hypnotized into believing something so insidious that it has jeopardized your ability to live the life you *deserve.* You have been lured into a lie that has controlled your mind and contaminated your life, a lie that has prevented you from being your best, from taking risks, from having the confidence and strength needed to seize the life that you've always wanted."

The wizard's voice had been building in passion, and he nearly fell off the stool at the end of his sentence.

"Friends," he said moments later, scooting back again to the center of the stool, "forgive my passion. But this spell is powerful, and you must be made aware of it. Though you cannot recall it ever happening, a spell has been cast upon you, and it has mesmerized you into believing that *you are not good enough* and that *there is something wrong with you.* This spell is Society's Spell, and it has made you secretly feel inadequate, ugly, weak, slow, small, useless, and helpless for far too long. Tonight *we break that spell.*"

The wizard paused and examined the crowd once more. Everyone was pressed to the backs of their seats; the force of the wizard's words had rolled over us like a great wave.

The wizard took a deep breath and eyed the ground. He spoke in an apologetic tone. "Unfortunately, I lack the power to break this spell on you. I don't have the time or the skills to completely break Society's Spell—you have unwittingly allowed it to control your life for too long, and my time is almost up. But there is good news," he said, his voice lifting. "*You* can begin to break the spell tonight, with this journey. Since you are the only one who can truly control your mind, you can defeat the spell. How do you break it?"

Now he slowly shifted to the edge of the stool.

"First, you must recognize that a spell exists. This one is easy. Look to little children. Watch them play and crawl and be. Does any child believe there is something wrong with himself or herself? No. Do small children routinely, if ever, experience the onslaught of negative emotions like insecurity, doubt, sadness, or depression? No. You see, you weren't *born* feeling badly about yourself, you were taught to feel that way. Here's more fundamental evidence. If, when I say to you, 'You are not good enough,' you do not have a *strong* reaction, a need to fight and argue with me or at least to scoff at me and brush me aside, then there is a spell on you. And it is neutralizing your innate desire to stand up for yourself and become the person you were destined to be.

"If you can believe this, then you have taken the first step . . . and you will be able to take the second and third. The second step is to interrupt the spell—to question or tune out society's messages, as well as those in your mind, that make you question your strength. The third step is to start living your life by conscious control. In your adventure here, you will take these steps and we will help you."

The wizard slowly tottered to his feet and shuffled to the front of the stage.

"Clearly, there is much ahead of you tonight. But now I simply want to impart an old magician's secret: to break a spell, you must override it with a more powerful magic. If you want to break Society's Spell, you must mix a magic within you that can overpower it. That magic, which I am sure you have long forgotten to stir within your soul, is *hope.* You must flood your entire being with the hope that you *can* start anew, that there *is* more out there for you, that you *will* become the powerful person you were destined to become."

He moved to the very edge of the stage and leaned out toward us.

"Of course, to many of you all this might sound like nonsense, this idea of a dark spell and a potion of hope. That's okay. It won't be until the end of your journey that you will understand how far away you are now from where you could be. Hindsight, they say . . ."

Two light, quick taps to my left shoulder diverted my attention from the wizard. I looked left and saw the small girl who had accompanied him onto the stage. She motioned for Henry and me to stand and follow her. "Hurry," she said, "you're not supposed to be here."

The girl led Henry and me down a long, dark hallway carved from the limestone bedrock behind the stage. We arrived at an oversize wooden door, and she motioned for me to open it. Inside, a damp, dark room sat unfilled except for a wooden bench.

"Sit," she said. "I'll fetch the wizard."

A few minutes later the wooden door opened with a crash, and the wizard entered out of breath.

"Henry," he asked, seemingly upset, "where is this man's invitation?"

Henry instructed me to give the wizard Mary's envelope, and I obliged, confused.

The old man peered at it closely, gave Henry a quick, startled look, then returned his attention to the envelope. He began nodding knowingly and looked up at me with tears in his eyes.

"Young man," he said, "are you ready to hear Mary's story?"

5
THE FERRIS WHEEL

The wizard led Henry and me through another long, dark limestone corridor. We came to a stairway that led upward to two large wooden doors, like the doors of a stone cellar. The wizard opened the portal, and we emerged about thirty yards to the right of the Ferris wheel. The ride was no longer moving or occupied with riders. The park was once again deserted.

"Where did everyone go?" I asked.

"On to their own adventures," the wizard said, glancing up. "Looking for answers." He turned to me and asked, "What answers are *you* looking for?"

The questions that had been building inside me burst out like machine-gun fire: "What is this place? What happened to Mary? Why did she want me to come here? Why did she mention her brother on her deathbed? How did my mom . . . the Truth Booth. . . . What's in the envelope?"

The wizard held up his hand, silencing me. "Good enough. Good questions. The answers will come." He looked at me curiously and said, "Tell me, do you believe that this is all happening?"

I thought about all that I had experienced so far. It felt like a dream. I shook my head. "No."

Henry let out a sigh and looked to the ground, as if disappointed in my reply.

"Strike one," the wizard said sternly. "When you arrived here, you signed a contract. That contract is everything. You agreed that you would be open to experience and possibility, but your response shows that you do not accept what is happening, which tells me you are not open to possibility, which tells me you care little about the contract. This *is* happening to you. Mary *was* hurt. You *did* speak with your mother. You *are* standing here with an old wizard and a gentle groundskeeper. And you *are* in danger of being asked to leave because you just broke your contract."

The wizard's eyes turned cold, and he stared at me expectantly.

"I . . . uh, I'm sorry, I just . . . this is all over-whelming, and I don't know how to . . ."

"Fine," the wizard said, cutting me off, "just hold your doubts and don't break your con-tract, or you're gone. Clear?"

I was stunned by his harshness. Where was the kind old man so full of hope?

"Got it," I said, confused.

"Glad we got that out of the way." He turned to Henry and winked, then smiled at me. "Be-cause I bet you're really not going to believe what happens next."

Henry and I boarded the Ferris wheel, and the wizard lowered the safety bar across our laps.

"Ready for a little magic?" the wizard asked, his eyes sparkling once again as they had in the cavern.

"Sure," I said without meaning it. I hadn't been on a Ferris wheel in years. Not since I met Mary.

The wizard walked off the operator's plat-form and stood in front of the Ferris wheel.

Lifting his right hand, he pointed his finger at the ride, slowly following the outline of the Ferris wheel with his finger. He appeared to be drawing counterclockwise circles in the air. He started speeding up the circular motion, going faster and faster. I saw him close his eyes, and at that precise moment a light began to emanate from his hand.

Suddenly, the ride lurched to life.

Henry and I were pushed forward into the safety bar as our cart swung backward.

"Holy—"

"Hang on!" Henry said, cutting me off and laughing like a child. "Here we go!"

Our cart swooped backward and upward. The Ferris wheel was in motion and moving fast.

"Whoopee!" Henry cried. His eyes sparkled with the excitement of a child.

We rose higher and higher, and the full expanse of the park revealed itself. The moonlit view showed the park to be much larger than I had thought. A square walkway formed the perimeter. I could see kiddie rides and game booths surrounding the square, then food huts and a large grassy area, a pirate ship, a carousel, and a gigantic metal barn. On the inside of the walkway stood a massive, circular tent, painted red and blue and gold, and dozens of smaller tents and walkways, more food huts, bumper boats, roller coasters, and dozens of other rides.

When we hit the top of the ride and started down the other side, Henry said, "Quite a view, isn't it?"

"Yeah," I said, in awe.

As we neared the bottom of the ride I looked to see the wizard, still making circular movements with his arm. When we made eye contact, he speeded up the motion. Our cart once again leaped backward, and I grabbed frantically at the safety bar.

"Not a fan of the Ferris wheel, huh?" Henry asked with a broad grin.

My knuckles were bone white on the safety bar. "No, not exactly."

"Why not? Seems fun to me."

"Yeah, I guess it is for most people. But I've heard stories about these rides." This very ride, in fact.

We were traveling only about one and a half times the normal speed, but that was too fast for me.

Henry huffed, "Nonsense, these things are very safe. What stories have you heard?"

I looked at him nervously. "I guess only one. The story of a little boy who fell off this ride. Mary's brother."

Henry looked at me flatly. "And what do you know of that story?"

"Well, not much. . . . Mary never really talked about it, and I never really asked. But I do know he fell to his death. So that's why I'm a little anxious up here."

"Seems like a story she would have told you about. That's a pretty big life event, losing your brother. And you say Mary was your fiancée? Tell me, how much of Mary's life story do you *really* know, then?"

He asked the question at the top of the ride, and as we began our descent I felt my heart fall as well. Mary had never been one to talk much about the past. Whenever I asked about her life growing up, she would just say, "Oh, those are boring stories, and anyway, the past is just the past. Let's live for today." She always said that, and her face lit up with an optimistic glow.

As we neared the bottom I turned to Henry and said, "I guess I never knew her life's story too well, but I always knew *her* well enough. We connected like *that.*" I snapped my fingers.

We passed the bottom platform, and the ride came to a sudden, screeching stop. Our cart tipped forward and nearly dumped me out. I looked wildly toward Henry, but he sat calmly, as if nothing had happened. The wizard stood still, holding his arm in one place. I looked back to Henry, and he nodded for me to look forward.

Two children boarded the cart in front of us.

One was a small boy. The other was a small girl . . . Mary.

The wizard moved his hand, and the ride lurched to a start once again.

I couldn't take my eyes off Mary's younger self. She looked exactly as I had seen her in childhood pictures: brown hair in pigtails, pink dress, black glossy shoes with neatly folded white socks, smile a mile wide.

As we rose higher the two kids talked excitedly and began tickling each other. When their cart was beneath us and I lost my view of them, I gave Henry a worried glance.

"Sometimes," he said, "we think we know a story, but maybe we don't know the *full* story." He turned around and looked at the cart behind us.

Todd, Mary's brother, was winning the tickle war. He raised both arms above the safety bar in victory.

My heart sunk as I realized what was about to happen.

"*NO!*" I screamed. "*I don't want to see this!*"

Mary leaned over Todd and pointed out their parents walking below.

I sat horrified, looking up to the kids' car as we descended.

When Mary and Todd's cart passed the loading platform, they yelled down happily to the people waiting in line.

The people in line—where did they come from?

We rose once more to the top of the Ferris wheel, and I saw that the park had come to life again. There were hundreds of people below. I heard the roller coaster in the distance. I saw a barker handing over a stuffed animal at one of the game booths. The noise and sights distracted me for a second.

Then I heard Todd scream.

We were descending again, and as I looked up I saw him screaming and waving at his parents below. "Hi, Mommy! Hi, Daddy!"

We passed the platform, and I saw the operator arguing with a man at the front of the line.

Our carts rose to the top again, and I looked back to see that Todd had pulled his legs up and under the safety bar. He was kneeling in his seat.

Mary was grabbing at him. "Sit down!" she demanded.

"I want Mommy to see me!" Todd squealed.

I tried to scream at Todd to sit down, but no sound came out of my mouth. I looked to Henry, who was staring at something below. I followed his gaze. The man in the front of the line suddenly stopped arguing and pointed skyward. The operator looked up to see Todd leaning far over the safety bar, waving at his parents. The operator screamed, "Kid! Sit down!"

Mary was also screaming for Todd to sit.

"Hi, Mommy!" Todd screamed.

"*Todd!*" someone screamed below me. I looked down. It was the two kids' father, Jim. He and Linda looked up in horror.

I glanced back to the operator and saw him slam a big red button.

The ride jolted and slowed.

"NO!"

Todd's feet dangled just a few yards above and out from me. Mary was leaning over the safety bar, desperately trying to grab him. She had managed to get a handful of his shirt when he lost his balance and went over the safety bar.

"Toddy, I got you!" she cried.

"Mary, don't lemme go!" he wailed back. He had one hand on the bottom of the cart and was frantically trying to reach up with his other hand.

And then he lost his grip. His shirt tore away.

The crowd below screamed and scattered.

I watched his mother cradle him in her arms, rocking him back and forth.

"No!" she cried. "Not my baby . . . not my baby . . . please no . . . not my baby!"

Jim looked up toward his daughter, still leaning over the safety bar, still holding the scrap of Todd's shirt. "Mary," he called out, "what have you done?"

The Ferris wheel lurched again and stopped when Mary's cart reached the bottom. The operator's face was pained as he lifted the safety bar and let her out. She walked slowly down the platform's stairs and toward her parents, through the crowd, which parted before her as she walked. She stood helplessly as the paramedics pulled her mother away from Todd's limp body.

I buried my face in my hands. "*No more!*"

Henry gently touched my shoulder.

"Why? Why are you showing me this?"

Henry whispered, "Sometimes we forget that everyone has important moments in their life—happenings that forever affect them. This was one of the stories you forgot about every time you called Mary a 'control freak.'"

I looked at Henry, horrified.

He continued. "Could it be there's a reason she always tried to get you to behave in a certain way, to follow the rules?"

The ride kicked on again, and our cart swayed forward to the bottom position. Henry lifted the safety arm and stood up. "Sometimes we forget other people's stories. Sometimes we even forget our own. It's time you were reminded of a few of the most important ones."

Henry lowered the bar across my lap, walked off the platform, and stood next to the wizard.

The wizard lifted his arm, and the ride lurched into motion. I watched his arm move faster, the ride moving with it. He circled faster and faster, and the light from his arm grew brighter and brighter. The ride began to squeal with noise as it spun. Faster. I grabbed hold of the safety bar. Faster. The wind rushed against my face. Faster. The view became blurred. Faster. The ride started to shake and shudder.

Too fast! Stop!

Suddenly I felt as if the ride was at normal speed again, but the view around me was still spinning and blurred and muddy, as if everything else were moving at a hundred miles an hour.

And then images started to appear against the dark, blurred backdrop: scenes from Mary's life.

She's at her brother's funeral, standing next to her mom and dad. No one is holding her hand.

She's in high school now, and a girl screams at her, "Ugly brace-face!"

She's sitting at a restaurant table, and her first fiancé says, "I'm seeing someone else."

She's at another dinner table, arguing with me now over a visit to her parents, and I say, "Why should we go? They don't seem to like you anyway."

The backdrop changes to the color of cotton candy.

Mary is playing with her brother on their front lawn.

Mary's mother is teaching her to play the piano.

Mary's dad is holding her hand and swinging her up and down as they walk into an ice cream shop.

Mary finishes a presentation, walks out of a room, and gets a high five from her co-workers.

Mary lifts her hand to her face, breaks into tears, and says, "*Oh, my God, yes, I will!*" as I kneel nervously before her.

Then the Ferris wheel stopped.

I sat at the top of the ride. The blur was gone. The images were gone.

I looked down to the wizard and Henry. The wizard started moving his arm in a circular motion again, this time in the opposite direction. The ride shuddered to life. Faster . . . faster . . . faster. The view blurred again. Snapshots appeared against a muddy-colored background: *snapshots of my life.*

I'm six years old, huddled on the couch, crying for my father to stop hitting me with his belt.

I'm twelve and standing at the side of my grandfather's hospital bed as he gasps for one more breath.

I'm sixteen, watching my mom beg the school principal not to expel me for punching another student.

I'm older now, receiving news from a stuffed shirt that I will be laid off in two weeks.

I'm in the kitchen, watching Mary slam the door behind her.

The blurred backdrop turns the color of lemonade.

I'm eight and jumping up and down with Mom on the trampoline in the backyard.

I'm thirteen and laughing as Grandma and I pet one of her horses.

I'm crossing the finish line first at a high school track meet.

I'm older now, shaking hands with a co-worker after leaving my new boss's office.

I'm signing the mortgage for my home.

I'm holding Mary in my arms, breathing a sigh of relief that she has agreed to be my partner for life.

And then I was back on the ground, standing next to the Ferris wheel.

Henry greeted me with a smile. "How was the ride?" he asked, his voice warm and soothing.

I shook my head, not knowing how to respond.

For a few moments I watched the rhythm of the crowd: parents chasing their children, clowns selling balloons, everyone laughing and walking as if it were a regular Saturday evening at the amusement park.

"Why did I have to see all that, Henry?" I asked, nodding toward the machine.

"What did you see?"

"Scenes from Mary's life. Scenes from my own."

"Oh, yes," he said as if he had forgotten a well-laid plan, "scenes from both Mary's and yours. Whatever you saw from Mary's life you must remember—you'll need that information later on. Whatever you saw from your own life was a reminder. Too often we forget the most important and meaningful chapters in our life's story. The scenes you saw were chapters like that. Important. Influential. They were the chapters that not only illustrated a few highs and lows in your life but also epitomized powerful *themes* that have become woven throughout your story."

"What themes?" I asked.

"Themes present in what you were taught in life, and themes present in how you have lived your life. We have to talk about those themes because, frankly, the themes in *your* life are a big part of why Mary ended up here . . . and in the hospital."

6
THE PARK'S THEME

Henry and I sat on a park bench some twenty yards in front of the Ferris wheel. The bright lights of the ride barely reached us. Henry leaned back on the bench, legs crossed and elbows resting on the backrest, just watching people saunter past. He didn't say a word to me for several minutes.

Finally, I could contain my frustration no longer: "You said the themes in my life were a big part of why Mary came here. So let's get on with it—which themes are you talking about?"

Henry looked at me with patient eyes. "I know you want a lot of answers, and you want them now. But I'm afraid that's not how this place works. You have to discover the answers for yourself. To know which theme in your life's story might have caused Mary to come here, you've got to discover which themes are woven throughout your story."

"And how do I do that?"

"You start with the scenes you saw on the Ferris wheel. Like I said, you saw those scenes for a very specific reason—not just to help you remember the bad times and good times, but also to help you uncover the dominant themes in your life's story. Patterns of what you have learned and how you have lived your life. Let's just talk right now about the first few scenes you saw. Then I'll help you figure out the themes that weave through-out them." Henry nodded at the Ferris wheel. "What was the first thing you saw up there?"

I looked toward the ride. A line of happy kids and adults were waiting their turn. Their patience didn't match the scene I saw in my head.

"The first thing I saw was an image of my dad. He was . . . angry."

"What was he upset about?"

"Me. I did something I wasn't supposed to."

"What was that?"

"I ruined the remote control to the television." Thinking about how trivial the incident was, I almost laughed. "We had a fish tank. I thought the remote would make a good submarine."

Henry chuckled. "Did it float?"

"Not even close. It did what submarines are supposed to do. It sank to the bottom. My arms were too short to reach, so I went to the closet and grabbed a wire coat hanger and tried to fish it out. But I got distracted and tried to fish out a fish. Dad walked in and there I was, holding a fish in my palms, standing on a stool above a tank filled with nervous fish, a coat hanger, and his remote control."

Henry laughed again. "So what'd your dad say?"

"Not much. He screamed at me for being a pest and came storming toward me. I got so scared I dropped the fish. As he got closer I panicked and jumped off the stool to get away from him . . . and landed on the fish. I remember looking up at my father in horror."

"You landed on the fish! What was your dad's reaction?"

The image of my father's furious face flashed in my mind.

"He said, 'You stupid little shit! Look what you've done!' Then he unbuckled his belt. I tried to get away from him, but he pinned me on the couch and . . . well, anyway, that's the first image I saw on the Ferris wheel."

I stared off into the crowd. Henry let a few moments pass. The kids on the Ferris wheel seemed so happy.

Finally, Henry said, "I know it's not easy to talk about that sort of thing—I've had some experience with it myself, so I appreciate your telling me about it. I know that happened a long time ago, but if you could go back and step into your young mind, what did you begin to think about yourself at that time?"

"*Think* about myself?" I asked reflectively. "I don't know. I guess I just thought I was an idiot, a pest."

"An idiot and a pest?" Henry asked. "So did you change your behavior after that incident?"

"Sure. I just stopped being a pest. I kept quiet and stayed out of my dad's way. That's what you do with a tough dad."

"How'd that work, staying out of the way? Did the abuse stop?"

"Sort of. I mean, when I was out of his way, there wasn't a problem."

"Were you scared of your father?"

I laughed. "Who *isn't* scared of their father? I think a lot of people grow up like I did—the world isn't full of rainbows and Ward Cleavers, you know. Listen, do we really need to psychoanalyze this? I know what my dad did was wrong, and I got over it a long time ago. Do we really need to talk about it anymore?"

"No," Henry said softly, "not right now. But understand that you saw that scene because it undoubtedly became a theme in your life in some way. Let's move on. What did you see next?"

I told Henry about my grandfather's death. He had suffered for weeks in the hospital, battling liver cancer. My family visited him often, especially in his final days. My dad would work to keep the visits lighthearted, but the second we walked out of the hospital he would curse Grandpa for his years of drinking. The night before Grandpa passed away there was an argument. Dad didn't come back the next day, because he was so angry. As Grandpa began to die I was the only one in the room; Mom had gone to call Dad and beg him to come. Grandpa's last words to me were, "You tell your dad I forgive him and that I always loved him." I stood crying as he wheezed his final breath. A nurse came in when the buzzers went off. She saw me crying but didn't say anything. She just unplugged Grandpa from the machines, pulled the sheet over his head, and told me to leave the room. Later that night I told my father about Grandpa's last words. Dad looked at me and teared up. Then he smacked me to the ground and called me a 'lying little shit.' He said I had made it all up to make him feel better."

"How old were you when that happened?" Henry asked.

"Twelve."

"What stands out to you about that incident?"

"Just how sad I was when Grandpa died. How uncaring and cold the nurse was. How Dad didn't believe me."

"At the time, why did you think your dad didn't believe you?"

"I think I just thought I was a bad kid, a bad communicator. Like I couldn't even explain what Grandpa had said to me."

"Did your relationship with your dad change after that?"

"Yeah. We grew even further apart. He never mentioned Grandpa again. Neither did

I. As a matter of fact, we never mentioned much of anything to each other after that."

I looked to Henry for his next question, letting him know I was ready to move on.

"Okay," he said, picking up on my signal. "Next scene?"

"The next scene was from my sophomore year in high school. I was one of the smallest guys on the basketball team. But not *the* smallest. A kid named Jimmy Smeltz was two inches shorter. We called him 'Smally.' He and I took a lot of guff from the older varsity players. We were only redshirts, and they were sure to let us know we were below them. One day I walked into the locker room and found Smally tied up naked to one of the metal posts in the communal shower. He was gagged with a sock and duct tape over his mouth. Tears streaked his face above the tape. I grabbed my pocket knife to cut him loose. As I bent down to cut the rope from his ankles, Clark Jones, our point guard and the most popular kid in school, snapped a picture, capturing me and Smally in an awkward position. Clark said he was going to print the picture and plaster it all over school. I tried to get the camera, and when he wouldn't give it to me, I broke his nose. An hour later my mother pleaded with the principal not to expel me. I received six weeks of in-school suspension and was kicked off the team. Clark Jones went un-punished and won us a championship. My mom took my side and told me never to blindly trust a person of authority again. Dad just ignored me and called me a trouble-maker from then on."

"You must've thought the world was pretty unfair after that," Henry said.

"I think I knew long before that."

"So what stands out to you about this one?"

"Just how damn mean people were. To tie Jimmy up like that. How bad was that for him? Man. And then for the principal to punish me and not Clark? That was ridiculous. Goes to show that if you stick your head out to protect yourself or others, you're going to get whacked."

"Did you do what your mom told you?" Henry asked.

"What's that?"

"Not trust authority figures again?"

"In a way. I definitely made people earn my trust."

"Did many people ever earn it?"

"No."

"Why not?"

The next scene popped into my mind. "Because you can never really trust anyone. Wait till you hear my next story."

The fourth scene I saw atop the Ferris wheel had taken place in a white, cold office. A consultant was sitting in front of me, thanking me for my eight years of hard work. Unfortunately, he said, my salary was too big a burden on the company, and I had to be let go. I was being replaced, he said, by a cheaper resource. I asked who would take my place, thinking that Benny, one of my senior managers for the past five years and now a new dad, was ready and deserving. Instead, the consultant coolly told me my job was being outsourced to a twenty-one-year-old in India. "Don't worry, though," he said. "We're offering a very nice severance package for people who gave so much to this company." I got six weeks' pay. Two days later Benny was laid off too.

"How's that grab you for fairness and trust?" I asked Henry. "I gave them eight years of my life, and they gave me six weeks and a slap in the face. Goes to show, you never know what's going to happen."

"You think it was unfair—a slap in the face—to be laid off?"

"You better believe it. I was so pissed off. It was like I wasn't valuable enough for them to pay me, or even have the decency to offer a pay cut. They just replaced me with some kid. How unlucky can you get?"

"Sounds like you're still upset about it."

"I am," I said peevishly. The more I thought about it, the more my blood boiled.

"Okay. So let's not get stuck there. What did you see next?"

The scene that played next in my mind cooled me down instantly, flooding my senses with sadness.

"I saw Mary slamming the door behind her," I said, feeling a lump growing in my throat. "I couldn't believe she had left. I just stood there. I didn't say anything, didn't *do* anything. I knew she was unhappy, but I didn't know just how unhappy. I knew she felt like we weren't heading anywhere. I think she always thought she'd marry someone who made her feel better. A few months after we got engaged I think she came to the realization that I might not be that person. I wasn't good enough for her. And in the last few months it was like she really got intent on

changing me. When I didn't get with the program, she became more and more upset.
And then she slammed that door and disappeared."

"Do you really believe you weren't good
enough for her?" Henry asked.

"Yes. No doubt. Mary was always an angel
to me. I just . . . I wasn't an angel back."

"What did you think when she didn't return, when she disappeared?"

"I immediately thought something was
wrong. I was always bad luck for people. All I
could think of was all the terrible things that
could've happened to her, all because I
pushed her away. And something terrible did
happen. She . . ."

I stopped and looked Henry in the eyes,
remembering suddenly why we were talking
about all this. "You said this all has something to do with the themes in my life—so
what themes do you see?"

"You want to know?" Henry asked.

"Yes."

"Okay. Let me reflect back to you what I've
heard, and let's see if we can figure it out. I
think there are some powerful patterns weav-
ing through the scenes you just described to
me. Let me give you my take. First, there

might be a theme to what you've been taught *about the world.* I think you've learned that the world is a pretty dark place. As you said when talking about your dad, 'The world isn't full of rainbows and Ward Cleavers.' Your father's abuse taught you that the world was a dangerous place; your grandfather's passing taught you that the world was a sad place; you learned that the world was unfair from your high school principal—that if you stuck your neck out, you'd get whacked; your layoff taught you that the world was unappreciative and uncertain; when Mary disappeared, you learned the world was out to get you—after all, you were 'always bad luck for people.' Am I on track so far?"

I nodded.

"Okay, I think there's another theme, this one concerning what you learned *about other people.* Your interactions with your dad taught you that other people were unkind, hurtful—that there weren't a lot of dads like you see on TV. Your grandfather's nurse taught you that people were cold and uncaring. Your basketball teammates taught you that people were cruel; your principal taught you that they were unfair. The consultant who laid you off showed you that people were generally cool, even uncaring, about other people's circumstances. Mary may have taught you that people who love you might leave you if you're not good enough. Am I making sense?"

Another nod.

"Finally, I think there's a theme to what you learned *about yourself.* You came to believe you were an idiot and a pest because of your father. You thought you were a bad communicator after delivering your grandfather's message and getting smacked for it. You learned you were a problem child after standing up for yourself. Losing your job taught you that you were not valuable, and your relationship with Mary taught you that you were not good enough and that you were a lightning rod of bad luck for others. Is that about right?"

I stared at him, dumbfounded. "Yes," I said.

"So the themes that have woven throughout your story sound like this: the world is a dark and dangerous place; other people are unfair and hurtful; you yourself are inadequate. Now, let me ask you something. Do you think these themes might have affected how you lived your life?"

"Of course."

"Do you think you adopted a positive or negative mind-set?"

"Negative."

"Do you think you were more open with people or more closed with people because of your experiences?"

"Closed."

"Did you believe you deserved happiness and love, or unhappiness and heartbreak?"

The image of my dad smacking me to the ground after Grandpa's death flashed in my mind.

"Heartbreak, I suppose."

"Hmmm," Henry muttered. "So the people and events in your life taught you to be negative, closed off, and doubtful of your worth. That's a pretty good prescription for a tough life, huh?"

"I guess," I said, feeling myself close down even as I said it. It was also a prescription for running Mary right out of my life.

Henry stood up. "Well, if that's a prescription for a tough life, I gotta tell you something—you swallowed it whole. You let the themes in your life become your beliefs, and you let those beliefs guide your behaviors. You swallowed what the world taught you,

hook, line, and sinker, without ever question-
ing it. Now, maybe you were too young to
question those lessons then, but you
should've questioned, or at least revisited
them, as an adult. But you didn't, and it cost
you—big-time."

He must have seen the surprise on my
face.

"Sonny, I'm just calling it like I see it. You
want to know why you lost Mary?"

I stared at him blankly, afraid I already
knew the answer. Why would she want to
stay with a pessimistic, shut-off, moping
schmo like me?

Henry nodded as if he could hear my
thoughts . . . then he shook his head. "She
left because she felt even worse than *you*
did." He paused while his words sank in.

Worse than I *felt?*

"Why don't you come with me," he said.
"There's something you have to see for yourself. I can't explain it to you—it's too sicken-
ing."

7

THE SCREAMING CARNIES

Henry and I walked under the Ferris wheel, and images of Mary's brother falling from the cart burned in my mind. We wandered past several snack booths, a teacup ride, and a mini–roller coaster for kids. So many people were on the walkway that we moved at a snail's pace. The noise of the rides, screaming kids, and shouting barkers was overwhelming. For a few moments we were being pushed along by the crowd; then Henry grabbed my arm and pulled me to the side of the path.

"Look," he said, pointing with his thumb behind us.

I looked down a long, deserted red gravel walkway. On either side of the walkway were a half-dozen tented game booths. The fronts of the booths had stuffed animals and other prizes hanging from them. I could see carnies manning the booths. The scene felt odd—not five feet away, a stream of happy fairgoers filled the path behind us, but this walkway was just dead.

I glanced at Henry.

"Listen," he said.

Suddenly, a tidal wave of shouting voices hit me: *"Step right up, folks! Play the greatest game of skill ever invented! Everyone's a winner here! Shoot seven ducks, win seven bucks! Land five rings on a bottle, win a bunny for your honey!"*

The screams of the carnies were piercing. I looked around as the crowd of people just kept on walking by. No one even glanced down the walkway. It was as if they didn't hear the carnies at all.

"Look closer," Henry said.

Looking down the row of tents, I felt a creepy chill come over me. I recognized every one of the carnies.

In one booth was Mary's brother. In the next was her mom. Another, farther down, was manned by Mary's father. In one booth stood the girl I had seen scream, "Ugly brace-face!" at Mary in one of the scenes from the Ferris wheel. In another booth, Mary's former fiancé was hawking softball throws. In the last booth—I squinted, disbelieving at first—I saw . . . myself.

I turned to Henry, eyes wide, about to say something to him, when someone brushed past me and started down the walkway.

It was Mary.

She was dressed exactly as she had been when she walked out of the apartment, before she disappeared: black skirt, lovely blue blouse.

"Mary!" I screamed frantically. "Mary!"

I started toward her, but Henry grabbed my shoulder, stopping me.

"It's just an image, son," he said. "She's not really there."

That didn't stop me. I tore loose from Henry and ran toward her.

"Mary!" I shouted, "Mary!" But when I reached out to grab her shoulder, my hand passed right through her.

I jumped back and looked at her. She was so beautiful.

I reached out for her again; again I grabbed only air. I waved my hand in front of her. She couldn't see me—she was just staring wide-eyed at the booths.

"It's just an image!" Henry called out. "Look. And listen close."

I turned back to Mary and saw tears welling in her eyes. She was staring past me. I turned to see what she was looking at, and there was her brother, screaming at the top of his lungs, "MARY, DON'T LEMME GO! MARY, DON'T LEMME GO! . . . DON'T LEMME GO!"

Her mother was wailing, "NO! NO! NOT MY BABY! PLEASE, NOT MY BABY!"

Her father cried out, "MARY, WHAT HAVE YOU DONE?"

The scowling girl taunted, "UGLY BRACE-FACE! STUPID, UGLY BRACE-FACE!"

Her ex-fiancé yelled, "YOU'RE SO BORING. . . .I'M SEEING SOMEONE ELSE, MARY!"

The carnie who looked just like me shouted, "WHY SHOULD WE GO, MARY? YOUR PARENTS DON'T LIKE YOU ANYWAY!"

Suddenly, Mary collapsed to the ground next to me and covered her ears. "Stop it!" she screamed. "Just stop it!"

The carnies persisted.

"MARY, DON'T LEMME GO!"

"MARY, WHAT HAVE YOU DONE?!"

"STUPID, UGLY BRACE-FACE!"

"I'M SEEING SOMEONE ELSE!"

"YOUR PARENTS DON'T LIKE YOU ANY-WAY!"

Mary screamed, *"Stop it! Please stop it! No more . . . no more!"*

The walkway fell silent. I looked into the booths and saw that they were empty. I looked back to Mary. She was curled up on the ground, crying and rocking back and forth.

"Oh, Mary," I said, and kneeled down beside her. "I'm so sorry, baby, I'm so sorry." I reached out to touch her face, but my hand passed through her again and touched only gravel. I crumpled to the ground beside her.

Mary wiped the tears from her face and stood up. She looked at the booths, clearly surprised that they were empty.

I opened my mouth to speak to her, but the sound of whispers behind us interrupted me.

Mary and I both turned around.

In the booths behind us were more carnies. This time they all looked exactly like Mary, and instead of screaming, they were whispering.

Mary stepped forward, and I followed. As we neared one of the booths, the whispers amplified.

"Mary," one carnie said softly, "it *was* your fault. You should've held on to Todd tighter."

Another said, "You shouldn't have let him kneel on the Ferris wheel. That was dumb. . . . You killed your brother, Mary. You *killed* him."

Another looked at Mary compassionately and said, "You can't help it, Mary; you're just an ugly girl. Might as well accept it—you *are* ugly."

Another frowned. "You're boring, honey. You've never had much of a personality. . . . No one is ever going to love you."

Another murmured, "Yep, you're going to be alone forever."

Another Mary hissed, "They're right. You're ugly and you're boring and you killed your own brother and no one is ever going to love you because of it."

Mary's lower lip quivered, and she shook her head violently, as if this might make them all disappear. Then she put her hands over her ears and turned and ran.

I chased after her, but as she reentered the stream of people on the walkway, Henry once again took my shoulder.

"It's just an image, son," he said. "And I'm sorry, but she's gone."

~

I sat cross-legged on a patch of grass next to a lemonade stand, waiting for Henry. The voices of the carnies still echoed; the image of Mary crumpled on the walkway lingered in my mind.

"Here you go," Henry said, handing me a cold lemonade.

He sat down next to me, and we watched the crowd of people walking by.

Minutes passed.

The noise of the crowd had faded, and I could hear only the scolding, taunting, blaming voices of the carnies in my mind.

Finally, Henry spoke. "D'you know she's heard those voices in her head nearly every day of her life?"

"Really?"

"Yes, pretty much every day. Maybe the voices didn't always say those exact words, but they still got the message across. Those voices have been playing in her head over and over, and she's suffered guilt and inadequacy and fear of being alone her whole life because of them."

I shook my head. "I just didn't know. . . . Are they always that loud?"

"Not always. As you heard, sometimes it's a scream, other times a whisper. But for Mary, those voices are always playing, like a tape loop somewhere in the back of her mind."

"But . . . can't she stop them?"

Henry gave me a smile that was at once kind and uncompromising. "No more than you can."

"What do you mean?"

"You hear voices too—voices that scream negative comments to you, voices that whisper, 'You're not good enough.' Have *you* been able to shut them off?"

"I don't know what you're talking about."

"Really? Do we need to go back to the booths so you can hear a few voices screaming at you?"

"No." I shook my head vigorously. "No."

"Okay," Henry said gently. "Think about it. Do you ever hear a negative voice in the back of your head?"

"Yeah."

"Close your eyes. What does it say?"

I closed my eyes and thought for a moment. I heard a soft but insistent voice in my head, repeating all the same themes from my life: "Be careful, the world is dangerous. . . . Don't trust anyone. . . . Stay out of people's way. . . . You're an idiot, a pest. . . . You're not good enough. . . . You're a real jerk." A sea of negative voices washed over my mind.

Henry nodded. "Yep, you can hear them too. And they always talk to you at the least opportune moment—when you're about to try something new or when you're falling in love."

"How do I make them stop?" I asked.

"You tell me. If you could have sat down with Mary after she heard all those voices and ran away crying, what would you have said to her?"

"I'd tell her not to listen to them. I'd tell her to argue with them or tune them out. I'd tell her that her mom and dad were just reacting to the situation, that they didn't mean to blame her. I'd tell her that it wasn't her fault. I'd tell her that in school sometimes people say mean things about us and we can't get stuck on them. I'd tell her that her ex-fiancé was a fool and she should forget about him. I'd tell her that I . . ."

Henry looked at me patiently.

" . . . that I didn't mean to be such an awful jerk and a fool too."

"You think you behaved that way to her?"

I lowered my head. "Just like her ex."

Henry leaned in close. "Why do you think you acted that way to her?"

"I don't know. I didn't know about her past. I didn't know my words would hurt her like that. I don't know what I was thinking or doing. I just wasn't paying attention."

"Ah," Henry sighed. "Then I know just the person we need to visit next."

8
THE HYPNOTIST

Henry and I walked down the midway. The smells of hamburgers and pretzels and pizza and cotton candy wafted from the food huts crammed tightly on either side. I was too sick to my stomach over the things I had said to Mary to feel any hunger.

At one end, the midway opened into a wide grassy field, with little tents full of trinkets for sale dotting its perimeter. In the middle of the field sat a stage and two sets of bleachers. Recorded music bellowed from speakers on either side of the stage. When a man wearing jeans and a red T-shirt hopped onstage and announced that the show was about to begin, people browsing among the tents ambled over toward the bleachers.

"Are we going to watch a show?" I asked Henry.

"No," he replied. "You're going to be in it."

I stood outside a tent to the left of the stage while Henry chased down the man in the jeans and T-shirt. When they returned, Henry took my elbow and, without a word, walked me into the tent, which was bare except for a dark, elderly man, Indian perhaps, sitting on a metal folding chair. He wore a red embroidered waistcoat with a long, loose, collarless dress shirt underneath. His pajama-style white trousers were hiked up to reveal red embroidered shoes to match the waistcoat. His gray hair was cut short, and he was clean-shaven. He sat with his eyes closed, drawing in deep breaths.

"Harsh?" Henry whispered.

The man didn't respond.

"Harsh?" he said again. "Harsh the Hypnotist, I have an assistant for you."

The man opened his eyes and looked up at us. When he seemed to recognize Henry, his eyes opened wider.

"*Henry?* Is that you, old man?" he said, his inflection rising with obvious delight.

"It's me, old friend."

Harsh jumped from his seat and wrapped Henry in his arms. He towered over a foot above Henry but was much skinnier. "Old friend!" he shouted. "What are you doing here?" Then he abruptly pulled away, looking at me, then back at Henry. Concern was written all over his face.

"Henry, now just what *are* you doing here?"

"I've brought the kid in, to help him out."

Harsh seemed almost panicked. "Goodness, Henry! Do you know what that means? Is it time? Are you sure?"

Suddenly I remembered what big Betty had said at the entranceway, that it was a big deal that Henry was helping me out. Henry, too, had said it was a big deal, though he never told me why.

"What does that mean?" I asked. "What does it mean that you're helping me out, Henry?"

The two men just looked at each other as if I hadn't spoken.

"Geez," Harsh breathed, staring at Henry in disbelief. "You *are* sure."

Henry nodded.

Harsh looked at the ground and kicked the earth.

An awkward few moments passed. I felt as though I were on the outside of a big secret.

"Okay," Harsh said. "How can I help?"

The show started. After a brief introduction, Harsh bounded onto the stage like a teenager. The crowd of about a hundred clapped politely, the way crowds do when they're interested but have no clue who the performer is.

Harsh launched into his act: "Ladies and gentlemen, tonight you're going to be stunned by the power of your subconscious mind. You're going to laugh at your friends; you're going to learn to control your thoughts and actions; you're going to be *hypnotized!*"

The crowd clapped, harder this time, and a few people whistled. Standing to the right of the stage, I chuckled at the crowd. They were excited about being hypnotized?

Harsh asked the crowd to close their eyes and start counting back from fifty. He told them he was not hypnotizing them but just testing to see if they were able to *be* hypnotized. While they were counting down, he explained what hypnosis was, stressing the word *control* several times. ". . . You are the one in *control* of your mind. . . . If hypnotized, you will still be in *control* of yourself." At the end of the fifty seconds, Harsh asked who in the crowd absolutely believed they could not be hypnotized. "Who among you believes you are in complete *control* of your mind?"

About half the crowd raised their hands.

"Great!" Harsh said. "We've found our pool of volunteers!"

Harsh chose ten people—five men and five women—and asked them to come to the stage.

As they arrived, I told them to stand shoulder to shoulder, facing the crowd, just as Harsh had instructed me to do before the show.

Harsh looked at the ten people and asked, "Now, how many of you are shy? How many of you are truly embarrassed to be standing in front of the crowd right now?"

A skinny, short woman in a black skirt raised her hand. So did a heavyset woman in a red sweater and a tall man in a white jersey.

The hypnotist asked those three people to come to the front of the stage. "Now, everyone give a hand to these three brave souls."

The crowd clapped, and Harsh scanned all the volunteers' faces.

"Now, the truth is, I know that *all ten of you* are a little nervous right now," he said. "So tell you what: I want all ten of you to just close your eyes for a second and take a deep breath. . . . Good. . . . Now let it go. Good. Breathe in deep again and hold it: one, two, three, four. Now exhale slowly: one, two, three, four, five, six, seven, eight. Now, just calm yourselves down. Tune out all the nervous thoughts and just tune in to my voice. . . . Tune out all the thoughts running through your head. . . . Turn off your thoughts. . . . That's it . . . just listen to my voice. Now, release all the feeling in your body. Feel your face and shoulders and neck relax. . . . Good. No thoughts. No feelings. Now, pretend the crowd isn't even there. Right now you're completely alone on this stage. . . . Good . . . no thoughts, no feelings, just my voice."

He walked in front of the seven people at the back of the stage and brushed his hand on each one's shoulder as he passed. He said, "If you just felt a touch on your shoulder, I want you to stand still, eyes closed, breathing deeply for a while."

He walked back to the three people standing at the front of the stage and briefly touched each of them on the head. "If you just felt your head touched, I want you to pretend that the crowd is gone and you're safe and comfortable. You just hear my voice and you feel totally comfortable. As a matter of fact, you're better than comfortable—you *feel* like you're about to have the best sex in your life. . . . You *feel* absolutely *HORNY.*"

The crowd erupted in laughter. So did I. For some reason, his serene Indian accent just didn't seem to go with the word *horny.* The three subjects didn't seem to notice. Harsh motioned for me to come and stand behind the woman in the black skirt.

He continued. "As a matter of fact, you *feel* so good onstage right now that you think everyone on this stage is absolutely *sexy.* You believe that so much that if you should take your seat and I should ask you later on how the people on the stage look, you'd jump up and down and scream as loud as you could, 'They're *sexy!*'"

Harsh reached up to the woman's forehead, pushed her backward, and said, "You're in control."

The woman fell into my arms and opened her eyes in surprise. I helped her stand, and she turned and looked at me in confusion, wondering what had just happened. Harsh approached her immediately and said, "Well, ma'am, you were right—you're in complete control. I tried to hypnotize you and you just fell asleep! Luckily, my assistant caught you! How do you *feel* right now?"

The woman sprouted a huge grin, and her face turned a forbidden red. The crowd burst into laughter.

"Why don't you go back to your seat, my princess. Everyone give her a hand for coming up onstage."

The crowd obliged, and Harsh moved on to the other two. He did exactly the same routine: a push, an apology, a question that made them feel aroused. The crowd ate it up.

Motioning to the remaining seven people onstage, Harsh said, "Okay, now on to our lucky seven. They've been standing back here the whole time, unconscious, and missing out on all our fun. What do you think, folks? Should we invite them into the fun? Should we throw them a party?"

The crowd hooted and hollered.

"Good. So let's throw a party!"

A dance song exploded through the speakers, and colored spotlights showered the stage.

"Now, of course, at any party," Harsh said, "you've got to have some dancers. What do you think, folks? Are these people cut out to be dancers? How do they *look*?"

The skinny woman in the black skirt and the other two volunteers seated in the audience jumped to their feet and screamed, "They're *sexy!*"

The crowd burst into laughter.

The three suddenly looked around, unsure what had just happened, and immediately sat down, embarrassed.

The crowd erupted into more gales of laughter.

Harsh continued. "Oh, well, if the seven people up here onstage are sexy, I guess they'll be great dancers. Of course, we all know men are usually too chicken to dance, but maybe these four remaining men will play with us today."

Harsh touched three of the men on their heads and whispered something to them, leaving the fourth man alone.

"And we all know women are much better dancers," Harsh continued. "Women have much better rhythm than men, so I'm sure these three ladies are like *Madonna*—they really know how to *strike a pose.*" He touched the three remaining women on the shoulder and whispered something to them.

"Okay, folks, we've got our dancers. Unfortunately, since the men are just big chickens, it's going to take a lot for these three women to convince the boys to dance with them. You never know what could happen at a good party. Of course, we all know that at any party there's always that one guy who stands over by the punch bowl and refuses to dance . . . ." Harsh walked up to the fourth man, touched his head, and whispered something in his ear.

". . . But you never know, maybe even that guy will dance tonight."

The scene was set. The music blared from the speakers. The colored spotlights danced across the stage. The three men stood on one side, the three women on the other, while the other man stood alone at a table with a punch bowl. All seven were now conscious, staring at one another and wondering what was happening.

Harsh suddenly pointed to the group of women and shouted, "You're *Madonnas!*"

The women immediately broke into dancing. One woman did a vogue-like sequence, stoically moving her arms around her head; another shook like a stripper. The third woman danced rhythmically and made suggestive faces. They all looked ridiculous.

The crowd howled.

All the men onstage laughed as well.

Harsh chuckled into the microphone. "Now, wait a second, men—you're laughing at the women? I don't see you busting a move out there. What is this, a high school dance? You're a bunch of *chickens.*"

The men all put their hands in their armpits and started clucking. They kicked the ground, heads jutting out as if they had beaks, and moved jerkily about.

The man at the punch bowl dropped the cup he was drinking from. Eyes wide, he looked horrified.

Harsh pointed toward the strutting chickens and said, "What do you think, folks? How do our men up here *look?*"

Three people in the crowd jumped up and screamed, "They're *sexy!*"

I could hardly stop laughing.

One of the chickens suddenly approached the wallflower at the punch bowl and started ramming his nose into him, as though pecking him with a beak. The man jumped back and scrambled to the other side of the stage. One of the dancers intercepted him, though, and grabbed his butt. The man jumped again and bolted in the opposite direction, where another woman grabbed him lasciviously, pulling him close. She started dancing suggestively for him, and suddenly he didn't seem to be in such a hurry. Another woman came and danced behind him, sandwiching him between her and the other woman. The man grinned, then started putting his hips into it.

The crowd roared.

After the show, I waited for twenty minutes inside Harsh's tent. Finally, the hypnotist walked in, grinning.

"Sorry," he said. "I've been chatting with Henry for a bit. What did you think of the show?"

"I loved it—hilarious."

"Oh, good. Thanks."

"I couldn't believe how powerful your control was over them. Especially the shy people. They really screamed from their seats. Your mojo really worked."

Harsh laughed. "So why do you think it worked? Why did people do all those things they normally wouldn't do? Why would they do things they would be embarrassed to see themselves doing?"

"I don't know!" I said. "I was wondering the whole time how you did it!"

"Actually, it's pretty simple. Other than the hypnotic relaxation mumbo-jumbo, I essentially did only one thing up there tonight. I momentarily stripped the volunteers of their *self-awareness* by preventing them from being able to answer the question 'Who am I being right now?'" Harsh paused and chuckled. "You see, if they could have answered that question, their internal dialogue would have sounded something like 'Oh, my gosh, I'm acting like Madonna up here, and the crowd is laughing at me!' or 'I'm dancin' like a chicken in front of strangers!' or 'I'm screaming something embarrassing at the top of my lungs!' But you see, they couldn't answer that question because I took away their ability to do so."

"How? How'd you do that?" I asked.

"I simply took away the three reference points every person needs in order to be *self-aware*. First, I told them to stop paying attention to their thoughts and feelings. Second, I told them to stop paying attention to feedback from the outside world, to pretend the crowd wasn't even there. Third and most important, I told them who they were, in this case Madonna or a chicken."

"That's it?" I asked. "That's all it took?"

"That's it, and that's powerful. Think about it. If you are unaware of the world within you—your internal thoughts and feelings—and you are unaware of the world around you—how people perceive you and your behavior—then you don't have the ability to answer the question 'Who am I being right now?' Because you judge who you are at any point in time by your thoughts and feelings *as well as* by what other people are thinking and feeling about you. Follow me?"

"I think so . . . ." I paused to digest the discussion. "So you're saying that to be self-aware," I continued, "you have to know what's going on in your internal world and you have to know what's going on in the world around you?"

"Close," Harsh said. "Don't forget the third reference point. To be self-aware you also need to *know who you are.* You have to have an internal standard for who you are or who you want to be. This is the most important reference point in self-awareness. Think of it as a three-legged stool. You can know your internal thoughts and feelings. And you can get feedback from the world. But if you don't have an internal standard for who you are to *compare* that information to, you aren't self-aware. In other words, you have to take your thoughts and feelings and the feedback you are receiving from other people and you have to ask yourself, 'Are my thoughts, feelings, and behaviors *supporting* who I want to be?'"

Harsh examined my face. "Get it? Self-awareness is all about paying attention to the world within us and the world around us and then *using* that information to decide whether we need to change our consciousness or conduct, what we're thinking, or what we're doing. Does that make sense?"

"Sure. So tell me again how that allows you to make people dance like chickens."

Harsh and I laughed for a few seconds; then he suddenly got a serious look on his face. He looked at me quizzically, almost annoyed. "But listen, you know that you're not here to learn how to make people dance like chickens, right?"

I was taken aback by his sudden change in disposition. "Uh, yeah, of course."

He didn't seem convinced. "Before I walked in this tent, Henry and I had a nice chat. He told me about your situation, and I think you can take an important lesson from our conversation about self-awareness. Are you willing to listen?"

"Yes."

"You see, you're lucky. You have the gift of consciousness. Unlike the volunteers onstage, you *do* have the ability to tune in to your thoughts and feelings. You *do* have the ability to pay attention to how you're making others think and feel. You have the ability to define who you are. Because of these things, you have *always* been able to ask yourself, 'Who am I being right now?' and you have *always* been able to decide if that person was the person you wanted to be or not. Do you agree?"

"Yes."

"Good." Harsh's demeanor grew even more serious as he squared his shoulders, tucked his chin, and stared down at me with cold eyes. "Then it's about time you started asking yourself, 'Who am I being right now?' a little more often, don't you think? Henry told me what you said to Mary."

He took a menacing step toward me, as if he might knock me down.

"What?" I stepped backward.

"I heard what you said to Mary. About her parents not liking her very much."

He took another step toward me.

"*What?*" I was so shocked by his sudden aggressiveness that I couldn't seem to say anything else.

"All you had to do was think about what kind of person you were being to her at that moment. All you had to do was *pay attention.* All you had to do was look at the horror on her face when you said that to her, and then shut your mouth and apologize."

Harsh grabbed me by my shoulders and started shoving me toward the tent's exit.

His voice suddenly changed, and he no longer had an Indian accent. "Instead, you've always been a little coward, dancing all over Mary's self-esteem, still letting your daddy control your mind, scared as hell to love anyone."

Harsh pushed me violently through the tent flap. I landed hard on the ground outside.

He stormed out after me and towered above me. "Stop being a chickenshit and start being a man!"

I looked up in horror. Those were words my father had spoken to me the last time I saw him.

PART 2

PART 2

9
THE ELEPHANT'S LEASH

That's it. I'm out of here!" I yelled. I sensed that Henry was trying to keep up, but I wasn't about to slow down.

"Just one second!" he called out behind me. "Just wait!"

I marched away from the hypnotist's tent and back onto the midway, intending to leave immediately.

"Hold on a minute!" Henry yelled.

I charged through the crowd without looking back. "I didn't come here to get thrown around or brainwashed. Screw this place!"

Anger boiled in my gut, and I stalked off with a vengeance. I wanted out. How dare Harsh put his hands on me? How dare he give me a lesson in self-awareness, then throw me to the ground? How dare he echo my father's words by calling me a "chickenshit"? But, come to think of it, how did he *know* my father called me that? Was it a coincidence? No. Nothing was a coincidence in this place.

I peered over the rooftops of the food huts, searching for the Ferris wheel. I spotted it to my left and took a quick turn in that direction. I glanced back down the midway. No Henry.

I stopped in midstride. The crowds were gone again.

I stormed on and charged past the abandoned walkway where I had heard the carnies shouting at Mary, and then past all the kiddie rides.

Not a soul in sight.

I hurried under the Ferris wheel, past the park bench where Henry and I had sat, and into the open square with the flagpole. The emptiness of the entranceway struck me as eerie. I passed the flagpole and had almost reached the turnstiles when I heard someone yell behind me, "*Strike two.*"

The wizard. I turned around and saw him standing at the entrance of the tent with the cavern inside.

"You signed a contract. You agreed not to leave your host's side. Where is Henry?"

"I don't care where he is," I shot back. "And I don't care about that contract anymore. I'm leaving." I turned back around and stepped toward the turnstiles.

"STOP!" The wizard's voice boomed as if from the heavens. I felt its echo reverberate through my whole body. The hair on the back of my neck stood up. I turned back around.

The wizard's eyes pierced me with anger. "Come *here!*" he commanded.

My feet shuffled helplessly toward him. The closer I got, the less angry he appeared.

He looked at me compassionately. "If you were anyone else, I would let you walk out those turnstiles. I would let you go back to your life. I would let you forget that any of this ever happened. But I cannot do that."

"Why?" I asked. "What do *you* care?"

"I care for two reasons. One," he said, pointing to my jeans, "is that envelope you have in your back pocket. I'm afraid that envelope can never leave here again until we figure out what happened to Mary and why. Two, I care for Henry. He put his reputation on the line for you to get in here. He cares about you for some reason, and I don't want to see my old friend make such a sacrifice for nothing."

I stared at the wizard as if he had just spoken another language to me. "Why do you care about the envelope? Why can't it leave here? What sacrifice did Henry make by bringing me here?"

The wizard smiled. "You see, you still have questions. That is why you cannot leave. Your work here is not done."

"What work?"

"Your learning. Piecing together your story and Mary's. Settling things with the past. Making things right in the present. Planning a new future. These things you will learn in time."

"When?"

"That's up to you. I invite you to stay a little longer. Do you accept?"

We walked past the Ferris wheel and turned left between two candy-and-soda booths. The pleasant smell of cotton candy helped release the tension in my body.

"Tell me," the wizard said softly, "why were you about to leave?"

The image of Harsh standing above me fired my blood all over again.

"Harsh the Hypnotist. He got violent . . . pushed me to the ground. I won't take that."

"Harsh? He pushed you to the ground? Why?"

"I have no idea. He just pushed me down and . . . said something my dad once said."

"Really? What was that?"

"My dad once said, 'Stop being a chick-enshit and start being a man.'"

"How did you feel when he said that?"

"Who? Harsh? Or my dad?"

"Harsh."

"I don't know. Scared, I guess. I was lying on my back, and he was towering over me like a madman."

"Just scared?"

"Mad too. Steaming."

"Mmm," the wizard grunted. "It's not hard to be scared and angry at the same time. Why were you angry?"

"Well, for one, because Harsh was being violent. It just brought up old emotions of anger, the ones I felt in the situation when Dad had said those words to me."

"What was that situation like?" the wizard asked.

As we strolled past a row of small tents on our left and what the wizard referred to as the "Big Tent" on our right, I told him the story.

I was seventeen, a junior in high school. It was the middle of basketball season. I had been kicked off the team the year before, but my mom was throwing a backyard barbecue for me and a bunch of the guys anyway. It was a great day. We all had our girlfriends there. I was dating a girl named Jennifer. Dad was inside in the den, drinking as usual. When everyone left, Jenn and I sat on the bench on our front porch and talked for hours. We ended up kissing, my first real kiss. I was on cloud nine, but I'd soon be in my own private hell.

Dad called me into the house. I could tell by the sound of his voice that he was drunk. I told Jenn I'd be right back, then went into the house and glanced down the long hallway leading to the kitchen. I could see through the window that Mom was still out back picking up.

When I walked into the den, Dad jumped out of his recliner and stared at me, seething with anger.

"Why the hell haven't you helped your mother clean up the kitchen?"

"Dad, I was just outside with—"

"I don't want to hear your excuses. You're always full of excuses. Your mother just spent all day slaving to throw you this damn party, and you can't clean up?"

"Dad, I was just out front with—" I started, but before I could get the words out, he knocked me across my face with the beer can in his hand. I fell to the floor.

"You little shit! I told you I don't want to hear any excuses from you!"

He kicked me in the gut and hollered at me to get up.

As I tried to stand he screamed, "You've *never* appreciated your mother!" and slammed his beer can into my face again. I fell to the floor and curled into a ball as he kicked me again and again.

Finally, I heard my mother scream for him to stop. I looked up, and she stood between us, trying to calm him down. Jenn stood at the entrance of the den, horrified.

My mom drove Jenn home while I cleaned up my bloody nose and the kitchen. Dad, oblivious, watched television in the den.

Less than an hour later, the police were at the door. As my dad spoke to them and I watched from the kitchen, I figured that Jenn's parents must have called the cops. I hoped they would put the cuffs on him and lock him up forever. But they left quickly after arriving.

Dad walked into the kitchen, looking pale.

"Get the keys," he said. "You're driving us to the hospital. Your mom's been in an accident."

It turned out that after Mom had dropped Jenn off, a drunk driver had run a red light and slammed into her car.

She was in intensive care for six days. After I spent the first day in her hospital room, I could barely stand to visit her. The blood and the bandages horrified me. It tore me up to see her that way. Dad made me go the first three days, but I skipped the fourth and fifth and just stayed home crying. The fifth night Dad called home and asked me to come to the hospital and watch Mom so he could go get a drink. I told him no and hung up the phone. A few hours later he came home blotto and beat me until I couldn't move. He kept screaming at me, saying no real man would let his mother lie alone in a hospital.

"Stop being a chickenshit and start being a man! Go see your goddamn mother! You never did love her enough, you little coward!" By the time he exhausted himself beating me, I had decided to move out.

The next day I packed my things and went to Jenn's house to tell her I would be staying at a friend's house. Her parents answered the door. I asked to see her. They said she didn't want to see me, and they didn't want their daughter involved with someone like me.

Later I went to the hospital. All the nurses kept asking me if I had been in the car wreck too, since my face looked like hamburger from Dad's beating.

The doctors wouldn't let him or me into Mom's room in her last moments alive. They were trying to save her, and we'd have been in the way, I guess. When a doctor came out, he looked at me sadly and walked up to Dad. The doctor whispered in his ear, patted him on the shoulder, and walked back into her room.

Dad looked at me and shook his head. As he turned and walked away, I heard him say, "If you hadn't made her throw you that damn party..."

And that was the last I ever saw of him.

By the time I finished my story, the wizard and I had walked completely around the Big Tent. On the other side, a fence encircled an area used for the animals in the circus show. We leaned on the fence, and I squinted into some of the animal cages. I could see lions, seals, giraffes, tigers, and monkeys. A few feet away stood four elephants. A gigantic man in a dirty burgundy Henley and a cowboy hat tended to them. When he saw us lean on the fence, he smiled and walked over.

"Mr. Wizard," he said, tipping his hat and smiling broadly, "Good to see you—been a long while."

"It surely has, Gus." The wizard nodded toward the elephants. "How's the family?"

"Oh, they're doing just great," Gus replied, beaming with pride at his charges. "Getting smarter and stronger by the day. You know, I got Jo-Jo there to lift up the back end of a truck with his trunk the other day. Stronger and smarter by the day. . . ."

Gus looked past us suddenly and grinned. "Well, I'll be! Henry?"

I looked over my left shoulder to see Henry approaching. A pang of guilt shot through me.

"Heya, right back at ya, Gus," he said, leaning on the fence beside me. He glanced at me and nodded, then looked past me to the wizard, who was standing at my other side.

The wizard nodded, and an awkward few moments passed. Gus seemed to want to say something to Henry, but the wizard shook his head. I wanted to say something to him too: *I'm sorry.*

"Henry," the wizard finally said, "Gus here was just telling us about how smart and strong the elephants have gotten."

"Is that right?" Henry replied. He turned to me. "You know much about elephants?"

"Not really," I said.

"Oh. You might find them interesting. Gus, why don't you tell us about elephants?"

Gus grinned at the invitation. "Sure. I'd love to give you the rundown." He motioned at the elephant closest to us. "Take Jo-Jo there—he's a perfect example of a good, healthy adult elephant. Adult elephants go anywhere from ten to thirteen feet tall; Jo-Jo's twelve feet. From trunk to tail, he's longer than your *car*—about twenty-three feet. He weighs more than *four cars,* around twelve thousand pounds. He can lift eleven hundred pounds and could tear a small tree out of the ground with his trunk. In the wild, where his habitat would be a five-hundred-square-mile stretch of land, he could run about eighteen miles an hour. But he's not just strong and fast—he's smart too. Like all elephants, he has the largest brain size to body weight of any animal on the planet besides humans."

Gus clearly had a lot of pride in the animals and his job.

Henry scratched his head. "Tell me somethin', Gus. There's always something I couldn't understand about your elephants. You say in the wild they roam five hundred miles and can run almost twenty miles an hour?"

"That's right."

"And you say they can lift eleven hundred pounds and can tear a small tree out of the ground?"

"Sure. In the wild, these guys often uproot whole trees for food."

"So tell me something," Henry continued. "How is it that those elephants there stay in one place? I see they're all just tied to a stake in the ground with a tiny rope. Don't they feel compelled to rip that stake out of the ground and roam free?"

"Nah," Gus replied. "They gave that urge up a long time ago."

"What do you mean?" the wizard asked.

"Well, you see, those elephants don't think they *can* be free. See, when they were babies, we tied 'em up for the first time. Now, when we did that, you better believe they tried to break free. They made all sorts of fuss and noise and tried like hell. But they were too small and weak. The rope was too strong. Over time they convinced themselves they couldn't be free, and they stopped trying. They've always believed they were too small and weak to pull the stake out of the ground."

"Now I get it," Henry said, a knowing smile on his face. He looked over to Jo-Jo, shoveling hay into his mouth with his trunk. "Well, Gus, I can see it's about feeding time, so we'll let you get back to work. Thanks for the information. We'll see you soon."

Gus tipped his hat and went to feed the elephants.

The wizard turned to me. "So there's our lesson."

"What lesson?" I asked.

The wizard looked at me as if I were a little thick. "That maybe it's time you stopped feeling small and weak." He looked at Henry and then back at me. "Well, it's time I got going too. You keep learning—and stay with Henry. So long," he said and walked away.

I turned to Henry to apologize for leaving, but he spoke first.

"Listen," he said softly, "I'm sorry about Harsh. That was my fault. I pushed him to challenge you. Sounds like he went too far."

"Yeah . . . but don't worry about it." I paused awkwardly for a moment, not knowing what to say. "Harsh said something my father once said to me. How did he know those words?"

"The park works in mysterious ways," Henry said. "You hear what you need to hear sometimes. I know what happened with you and your father, what you told the wizard, and I think I have something you need to hear. Are you willing to listen?"

I was shocked that he knew about what I told the wizard. But that feeling passed quickly. Nothing surprised me too much about this place anymore. "I'm listening."

Henry nodded toward the elephants. "I think that you need to forgive your father and yourself and everyone else who has hurt you." He turned to me and spoke passionately. "You need to break free from the fear and suffering and anger that you have chained to the past. Because those emotions are holding you back from living freely. They're holding you back from venturing into new territories. They're holding you back from being who you were meant to be. It's time you used your smarts and your strength."

I shook my head. "I know, Henry. I know. It's just . . . that's easier said than done."

"That's why it's time for us to go see your father," he said.

10
THE PIRATE SHIP

I rushed after Henry as he walked away. "What? Did you just say we're going to see my father?"

"I did," he said. "Now, no more questions. Just come with me. And think about what you want to say to him."

We walked north, beyond the animal keep and back onto the main walkway that went around the park. The crowds were back. We kept walking, past a bumper boat ride teaming with screaming children, past a merry-go-round playing calliope music. Stopping on a sea-blue, crescent moon–shaped platform, we gazed up at a big wooden pirate ship. Two towers rose above the ship, one on either side; the ship's mast ran up to the height of the towers. Stairs rose up into a square entrance cut into the side of the hull.

Throngs of people passed behind us, and a knot of teenagers complained and cursed when they saw a sign hanging by a chain across the entrance: RIDE CLOSED.

Henry pointed up to the ship. "Think of it as a pendulum. Below the platform is a big wheel with a tire that spins against the bottom of the ship, giving it momentum, making it swing. Kids really like this ride. They sit in seats, and the ship swings higher and higher. We used to give them shields and swords and eye patches, but we quit because too many kids would throw the stuff overboard. Anyway, the ride is closed because they've taken all the seats out to sand the floor."

Henry called loudly up toward the entrance, "Willy! You in there, Willy?"

A man in a red bandanna and white-and-black-striped shirt leaned over the side of the ship. He wore an eye patch. "Ahoy, down there! Who be callin' me name?" Staring down at us, he opened his mouth in surprise, then pulled off his eye patch and squinted. "*Henry?*"

Willy unhooked the chain at the entrance-way, bounded down the stairs, and gave Henry a great bear hug, spinning him in circles. "Henry, you old landlubber! You've returned!" He let Henry loose and looked him in the eyes. "Then it's time?"

Henry nodded. "We'll talk later. For now, any chance you can teach this kid how to be a real swashbuckler?"

Willy eyed me up and down and smiled, revealing a few missing teeth. "*Aye!*" he cheered happily. He put an arm around Henry and the other around me and led us up into the hull of the ship.

The ship's deck was about twenty-five feet wide and fifty feet long—much bigger than I would have imagined. The entire deck had recently been sanded, and the floor was covered in dust and wood shavings. The mast rose in the center, and toward the stern a spoked wooden wheel four feet across rose from the deck. The only other feature of the deck was the hatch, a square hole on the starboard side that led to the belly of the ship below.

Willy strapped a wooden shield tightly to my left forearm with two thick, rough straps of leather.

"How's it feel, mate?"

"Fine," I said. The shield was wider than a large pizza, and definitely heavier, but it felt secure and oddly natural on my arm.

Willy showed me how to hold the shield and bow my head behind it to protect myself from an attack. "Keep your shield up," he said, "and you'll always minimize the risk of being hurt."

He offered me the hilt of a heavy wooden sword—it fit squarely in my palm. "Easy for a tight grip?" he asked.

I nodded.

He taught me how to squint around the shield and spot the weaknesses in an enemy's defense. He also showed me the best crouching position, one in which my legs were flexed, ready to leap forward and thrust my sword when my enemy was vulnerable.

"Always strike first and strike hard," he said. He spent about a half-hour teaching me how to block and thrust and parry and counterattack. A crowd of people had gathered below, wondering what was going on—they were able to view just the top half of our bodies.

"Okay, Willy," Henry said, watching us from behind the captain's wheel. "He's ready. Let's go."

Willy and Henry walked over to the hatch. Willy threw his shield and sword onto the deck and descended below; Henry started to follow.

"Hey!" I called out. "Ready for what? Where are you going?"

"It's time we left you alone," Henry said, "to fight your enemies."

Minutes passed, and I peered over the port side, down into the crowd. Henry and Willy were down there talking. I watched them for a moment until I heard something behind me.

I turned around . . . and froze in terror.

My father stood just in front of the hatch. He strapped Willy's shield onto his left arm.

I squeezed my eyes shut hard in disbelief.

When I opened them, he still stood there. He looked exactly as he had the last time I had seen him, when he walked away from me outside Mom's hospital room: black trousers, white dress shirt, sleeves rolled up, narrow black tie loosened around his collar.

I found myself moving toward him.

He adjusted the strap of his shield.

As I drew closer I could smell the stench of whiskey oozing from his pores.

He bent down, picked up the sword, and looked at me for the first time. His eyes glowed red.

"If you hadn't made her throw you that damn party . . ."

"*No!*" I heard myself scream, and I lunged at him with hatred. I forgot Willy's coaching and just tried to slam my sword down onto him like a hammer. He threw up his shield and blocked my sword, then kicked me in the stomach. I fell backward onto the deck.

He yelled and charged at me. "You stupid little shit, I'll teach you to raise a hand to me!"

I scooted frantically backward, pushing myself away with my hands and heels. In a flash he was on me.

As he pounded at me with his sword I instinctively blocked it with my shield, pivoting and kicking him in the thigh. He cursed and stumbled in pain.

I scrambled to my feet and backed up into the port rail.

Dad charged me again, yelling, "You *never* appreciated your mother!"

He swung at me, and again I parried the blow.

I heard the crowd below shouting and cheering, no doubt thinking they were getting a free show.

Anger exploded within me, and I screamed and charged, pushing him backward.

I hopped to his side and swung my sword wildly, striking him hard on his right arm, just below the shoulder muscle. He howled in pain and rage and swung right back, slamming the wooden blade across my left forearm.

Stepping into me, he bashed me full-force with his shield, sending me back into the railing again.

"Your mother spent all day slaving to throw you that damn party, and you couldn't even clean up!"

He stepped toward me once again, but I feinted and swung my sword in a wide arc, right across the side of his face. He fell to the ground screaming in pain.

I pushed myself off the railing and stood above him, and as he raised his shield I unleashed hell.

I swung my sword like a baseball bat, hitting him over and over again, pummeling his arms, legs, shoulders, ribs. "You son of a bitch!" I screamed uncontrollably as I kicked at him repeatedly. "You bastard!" I kept hitting, kicking, spitting, screaming, crying.

I beat him until I was exhausted and my voice was hoarse. Then I backed away, dropped my sword, and stared at him lying there.

He was curled in a fetal position, covering his head and neck with his shield. His chest heaved, and I heard his labored breathing. His arm and shield fell to his side, revealing a bloodied face.

I looked down at him, wishing he were dead. *"You ruined my life!"*

He blinked several times and shook his head from side to side, then sat up, wiping blood from his mouth. He looked at my sword on the ground and the shield next to him, then back to me with a face of exasperation. "I didn't ruin your life, son. I haven't seen you since you were seventeen. Your life is what it is because of you, not me."

I stared at him in shock. "No! You beat me! You ruined my life!"

Dad rose to his feet, grunting in pain. He bent down and picked up his sword, then limped across the deck with it and paused at the edge of the hatch. He threw the sword down into the darkness, took his shield off, and threw it down as well. Wiping the blood from his nose, he looked back at me sadly. "You were always full of excuses."

He took a few steps down into the hatch and looked back at me once more. "You're not small and weak anymore. You can't keep using me as an excuse to live shield up and sword out. Your life is what it is because of you, not me." Then he disappeared down the hatch.

I crumpled to the floor and sobbed uncontrollably.

A voice exploded from across the deck. "*Get up, you little pest!*"

I looked over and saw myself emerging from the hatch.

What the . . . ?

A mirror image of me stepped onto the deck. He wore the same clothes that I did. He stood the same way I did. He held the same shield and sword.

"You were always a little crybaby. Now get up, you little pest!"

I just stared blankly at him, thinking, *This can't be happening.*

"I said, *get up!*"

He suddenly bolted across the deck and kicked me viciously in the chest. I fell to my side and sucked in air.

"I *hate* you, you little shit!" he cried and started kicking me and swatting me with his sword.

I rolled up into a ball and protected my head with my shield.

He kept kicking and bashing at me with his sword.

"You freakin' loser!"

"You're such a failure!"

"Why don't you get your stupid ass off the couch!"

"You shouldn't have thrown that damn party!"

"It's all your fault!"

"You don't deserve a goddamn thing!"

Suddenly someone screamed for him to stop. I heard him back away from me and scream, "Just leave me the hell alone."

I peered around my shield and saw Mary standing at the edge of the hatch.

She looked at the man standing in front of her and said, "Why are you doing this to yourself?"

"None of your goddamn business!" he seethed and charged toward her.

I screamed helplessly from the floor. "*No! Leave her alone!*"

He reached her and drew his sword up above his head, ready to bash her.

Unfazed, Mary said, "*I love you.*"

He stopped in midswing and looked at her in horror.

"Honey, I love you," she said, this time softly.

He dropped his sword and shuffled backward. "No. No, you don't."

"Honey, I do."

He raised his shield and kept backing up. Mary followed him and tried to look around his shield.

"Why are you hiding? Why are you doing this to us? Why don't you tell me what's going on?"

"You wouldn't understand!" he fired back. "You can't understand me. . . . Just get away!" He backed into the bow railing and hunkered behind his shield.

Mary reached him and tried to push the shield to the side. "Honey, let me in. I love you. I just want to know what's going on with you. I need to know. . . . I need you."

He began to sob heavily and dropped his shield. "I can't. I can't tell you." He sobbed uncontrollably, and Mary took him into her arms.

"Why won't you open up to me?" she said. "Why are you so sad? Is your life . . . is *our* life . . . really that bad?"

Lying on the deck, I cried out, "No, honey, it's not!"

I struggled to stand up and winced in pain.

When I opened my eyes, they were both gone.

11
THE MERRY-GO-ROUND

Willy unstrapped the shield from my forearm. "You done with this, matey?"

I nodded with exhaustion.

"And this?" he said, grabbing the sword from my right hand.

"Yes."

"Good. Henry's over at the merry-go-round. He wants you to meet him there."

I shook Willy's hand and started down the hatch.

"'Ey, mate," he called after me.

"Yeah," I said, looking back at him.

"Don't worry. The dark waters will be blue soon enough."

Henry stood in a long line at the merry-go-round. When I joined him, he seemed not to notice me. He was staring thoughtfully, almost longingly, at the spinning ride. He closed his eyes and hummed along with the organ music that was playing in the background.

The ride came to a stop, and the operator unhooked the rope that held back expectant passengers. The line moved forward, and both children and adults hurried excitedly to find a horse. As we moved up in line, I could see that the horses were intricately carved and painted.

"They're gorgeous," I said to Henry.

"Hand-painted," he replied.

As we arrived at the front of the line, the operator stopped us and started the ride with the press of a button.

Henry turned to me. "You know, this is my favorite ride. It's so simple, so elegant, so beautiful. But most people overlook it. They're more attracted to the drama of the other rides. If you asked folks leaving an amusement park what their favorite ride was, most of them would say the adrenaline starters. The zippers and roller coasters and elevators that lift you up and drop you down. People remember the scary rides more than the pleasant ones. Sad, don't you think?"

"Yeah. I guess." I was still thinking about the pirate ship. About Dad. And Mary. And myself.

"Hey," Henry said, getting my attention. "You okay?"

"Yeah," I lied. My body felt as if it had been through a meat grinder, and my mind wasn't too much better.

"Listen," he said, "I know you've been through a lot. And I have to tell you, you're handling it well. You know, I've been thinking hard about your story for a while, about your life, about what I've seen you go through here so far."

He paused and looked at the merry-go-round.

"You remember the scenes you saw on the Ferris wheel?"

"Yeah." A few of the images popped back in my mind: my dad hitting me with his belt, Grandpa's death, Mom at the principal's office, getting laid off, Mary leaving.

Henry cocked his head sideways and looked at me quizzically. "I'm guessing you're

thinking about the first five scenes or so, am
I right?"

"Yeah? So?"

"So . . . so I think that's kind of sad. You
see, you're like most people. You're the type
of person to remember all the scary rides
and forget all the pleasant ones. The simple
ones. The beautiful ones. I think you've been
living your life focused on those first five
scenes and the dark themes they've repre-
sented. I think you've obsessed about the
experiences in life that dropped you to the
ground, and you've overlooked all those that
slowly and gently lifted you higher."

"What do you mean?"

"I mean, you've been returning to the
wrong rides all your life. Don't you remember
the other scenes you saw on the Ferris
wheel? The ones that floated above the
lemon-colored background?"

"Yes, I remember them."

"What did you see?"

I thought for a moment. "Well, I saw a
scene with my mom. We were jumping on
the trampoline in the backyard. I saw me and
my grandmother petting one of her horses
and laughing. I saw myself winning a race in

high school. I saw my co-worker shaking my hand after a promotion. I saw myself signing my first mortgage. I saw Mary. . . . We were hugging after I proposed to her."

"Those sound like good times."

"They were."

"Well, then, I have a quick question for you. Why didn't you let those good times influence you as much as you let the bad times?"

I stared ahead, unsure of what to say.

Henry smiled. "Let me help you with that. Remember how we talked about the themes in your life? We discovered that *some* of the themes that have woven through your life's story sounded like this: the world is a dark and dangerous place, other people are unfair and hurtful, and you yourself are inadequate. Remember that?"

"Yes, I do."

"Well, would you agree you've sort of lived your life under those themes? That for the most part you've lived your life pessimistically because of them, guardedly because of them, unsure of yourself because of them?"

I thought about what he said, and lowered my head. "Yeah, I would agree with that."

"Then I say again, I think that's kind of sad. I think there have probably been a lot of wonderful moments in your life that you could have focused on. I think there have been a lot of powerfully positive moments you could have let influence you. Moments that could have made you stronger, wiser, smarter, more compassionate and courageous. But instead, you focused on the dark times in your life, and you let them overwhelm you."

"Folks," the ride operator called out, interrupting Henry's speech and my thoughts. "Your turn."

The ride had come to a stop, and I hadn't even noticed.

"Go ahead," he said and waved us on.

"C'mon!" Henry said, and gleefully skipped toward the ride.

I thought, *Old men skip?* I limped after him, my legs still stinging from the sword blows, and we both climbed up onto the platform. Henry chose a horse and motioned for me to take the one next to him.

"I think I'll just stand this one out, I'm a bit sore."

"Nonsense!" he laughed. "This is going to be great! C'mon, you used to love horses. Jump on!"

The ride began, and Henry let out a loud *"Whoo-hooo!"* A dozen little kids echoed him. I would have joined in, but my legs and butt were screaming loud enough already—the hard wood of the horse's saddle was not pleasant against the welts and bruises.

The ride began, and the breeze felt wonderful on my face. The horses began to rise and sink on their brass poles. Henry hummed along with the organ music. The people standing around the merry-go-round waved at their loved ones on the ride.

For the first time since I entered the park, I felt at ease. The motion of the ride, the gently spinning platform, the horses rising and falling, everything was calming and soothing.

Henry let out another whoop and smiled broadly at me.

"Hey!" he said. "Look at me! No hands!" He lifted his arms in the air like an airplane and closed his eyes. *"Whoo-hoo!* Try it!"

I laughed at the sight of the old man. I lifted my hands in the air and spread my arms out wide. I laughed at myself and closed my eyes.

Whooosh. A strong wind hit me, and a brilliant flash of white caused me to blink.

C'mon, kiddo! Keep up!"

I opened my eyes and saw a woman galloping in front of me. The horse beneath me snorted, and I felt its powerful muscles flex to pick up the pace. A sea of open green field lay all around me.

"C'mon, kiddo!"

I shook my head so hard in disbelief that I nearly fell off the horse. Gripping the reins instinctively, I pulled them tight. The horse whinnied and slowed. As he stopped and I was pushed forward in the saddle by the momentum, I realized my legs didn't hurt anymore. I looked at my surroundings in surprise. The sun was about to set in front of me, and the sky was a purplish red. A range of mountains towered in the distance. The wild grass below me was thick, and the soil moist.

The woman riding in front of me turned around and galloped back toward me. I could see only her silhouette against the backdrop of the setting sun.

"Hey ya, kiddo," she said as she approached, "we're almost home. Plenty of time to rest after we get these guys into the barn."

She pulled her horse up next to mine, and I gulped in air on seeing her face.

It was my grandmother.

"Well, you look as pale as a ghost! You feeling okay? Need some water?"

She reached into the satchel behind her and handed me a canteen.

I was staring at her so intently that I didn't even reach for the water.

"Take some," she said and pushed the canteen closer toward me.

She looked young and vibrant, not at all like the last time I had seen her. She had died when I was nineteen, two years to the day after her daughter, my mother, was killed in the car accident.

"Let's get home. You look awful, sweetie! You must be hungry!"

She snatched the canteen, put it in the satchel, and gave a tight tug on the reins. Her horse wheeled around, and she told me to follow.

I pulled up next to Grandma's horse at the watering trough outside the barn. Grandma was brushing him down. I dismounted and petted my horse's neck as he dipped his head into the trough. I glanced into the trough and saw a thirteen-year-old boy looking back up at me.

"C'mere, kiddo," Grandma called.

I rounded the trough, and she pulled me into a wondrous hug. She squeezed me tight and kissed my forehead.

"You rode well today. Next time maybe I'll let you ride Thunder here instead of that old nag." She let me go and gently held Thunder under his jaw. "Here," she said, pulling his head toward me, "pet him on his cheek. He likes that." I petted him, and she said, "So, Thunder, what do you think—you think he's ready to ride a speedster like you?"

Thunder snorted, blowing back the hair from my forehead. Grandma and I laughed with dreamlike abandon.

After the horses were brushed and watered, Grandma told me to put them back in the barn. She pulled the saddlebags off Thunder and threw them over her shoulder. Then she gave me a boost up into his saddle. Adjusting the stirrups a little higher, she looked up at me warmly, tears welling in her eyes.

"Thunder here was your granddad's favorite. You sure look a lot like him sitting up there." She paused and fought back the tears. "He sure was proud of you. I don't know if I ever told you that. He loved you so much. He always said you'd go real far. Said you had a good heart, good character."

She brushed Thunder's neck and wiped away a loose tear. "I know things can be tough at home for you sometimes. Your mom told me what goes on. You call me if you ever need anything. No matter what, I want you to always keep your chin up and your heart open, okay? You're a good boy. You do what Grandpa always said: keep learnin' and livin'. You just learn as much as you can so you can be smart and happy, and you always live the life you want to live. You hear me?"

I brushed back the tears and nodded.

"Good. Now get those horses in."

She pulled Thunder toward the barn and gave him a pat on the hindquarters. He leaped into motion, and I almost fell out of the saddle.

"Whoo-hooo!" Grandma screamed excitedly. "Like riding a storm, isn't it!"

I snatched up the reins and gave Thunder a gentle kick with my stirrups. He burst into a gallop toward the barn.

"You're flying now, kiddo! Whoo-hooo! You're flying now!"

I let go of the reins and spread my arms out wide.

Whoosh! A blinding flash of light.

The organ music clued me in to where I was. I opened my eyes and lowered my arms. The merry-go-round was slowing to a stop.

Henry dismounted from the wooden horse and walked around mine. "You look good up there."

I felt my eyes stinging and tried not to cry. "Thank you, Henry."

"Anytime," he said with a grin, and started to walk off the platform.

I called after him. "Henry!"

He turned. "Yeah?"

"No, I really mean it. *Thank you.*"

12
THE HALL OF MIRRORS

Henry handed me a corn dog on a stick, and I tore into it greedily.

"I'd better grab you something more," he chuckled, turning back toward the hot dog stand. "Hang tight."

I waited for him outside the entrance to the Hall of Mirrors, where the occasional visitor wandered in or out. The attraction had stiff competition. Across the walkway were the bumper boats and a single-loop roller coaster called the Cyclone.

A few minutes passed, and Henry returned with two enormous puffs of cotton candy, grinning. "You only live once, right?"

We climbed the stairs to the Hall of Mirrors entrance, picking away at our treats.

"How you feeling?" Henry asked.

Strangely, all the pain in my body was
gone. "Uhh . . . good. . . . I feel surprisingly
good."

"You look a bit better. Maybe some weight
has started to lift off your shoulders?"

"Tons," I said, cracking a smile.

"Oh, good."

When we entered the attraction, a musty
odor swept away the sweet fragrance of the
cotton candy. The Hall's walls were painted
in once-garish zigzag patterns that had faded
long ago. The well-worn hardwood floors revealed the path taken by most of the visitors.
Filling the main room were a dozen or so
freestanding walls, from which hung various
oddly warped mirrors. Many of the mirrors
looked dusty at the top and smudged at the
bottom with children's fingerprints.

"A staple of any amusement park: the Hall
of Mirrors," Henry said, looking around. "Everyone expects to see it here. It doesn't do
that well, though, so the owners never clean
it up or spend anything to update its image."

We stood in front of a wavy-shaped mirror
that made our legs look short and squat and

exaggerated the size of our midsections. Eating our cotton candy and looking at the reflection, we had to laugh at ourselves. "Must've been the corn dog," I joked.

Another mirror made us look gigantically tall, with pinched waists and stretched faces.

"Why the long face?" Henry asked. I groaned.

In another reflection we appeared without midsections, just heads atop two pairs of oversized shoes. Finishing up my last bite of cotton candy, I motioned to Henry's reflection and cracked, "Your ego is really getting out of hand, Henry."

I approached another mirror and was surprised to see no image of myself at all—just the reflected wall behind me, and a couple walking by in the background, but no me.

I murmured, "Huh . . . ?"

"Look closer," Henry said.

I looked back to the mirror and still saw nothing.

"Closer," he said again. "Squint if you have to."

I squinted into the mirror, and a fuzzy image started to appear. As I squinted harder the image came into focus. It was me, squinting back at me. But it wasn't really a reflection of me. In the image I was shirtless, with a bad case of bed head. The background wasn't the Hall of Mirrors, but my bathroom wall at home.

I was watching myself watch myself in a mirror.

"This . . . is weird," I said, staring at the image.

The "mirror me" scratched his head and peered into the mirror. Turning on the faucet, he splashed water on his face, then stared back. He looked at the bags under his eyes and the wrinkles on his face. He stood sideways and let his stomach fall out, then sucked it back in, flexed his chest and arms, then let them go. He leaned in closer to the mirror and stared into his eyes, and with head hung low whispered, "God, you've become pathetic."

I watched him hop into the shower, get dressed, then sit silently over a bowl of cold cereal.

"How does he look?" Henry asked.

I couldn't stand the sight. "I look—*he* looks—tired, awful. Like he's half awake, and half . . . dead."

My mirror self walked back to the bathroom and brushed his teeth. In the bedroom,

Mary was still asleep. He let out a despairing sigh.

He went out the door and got in his car, where he listened to some trash-talk radio. At work, he walked by dozens of desks to his corner office without saying a word to anyone. His assistant came in and handed him a printout of the day's schedule. She was bubbly and bright-eyed. "Should be a big day, huh? You excited for the meeting?"

He didn't look up at her. "Not really." He didn't see her frown and shake her head sadly.

He sat quietly in his office, answering e-mail and gazing absently out the window. After looking over a sheaf of papers, he gathered them up and walked to a conference room at the end of the hall. As he entered, several people stood and shook his hand. He flashed a fake smile and joked around a few minutes about the weather and last night's NBA game.

"Hey!" I said, watching the scene in the mirror. "I recognize this meeting. This was about a month ago. It was a big meeting. We were reviewing the quarter and brainstorming what we could do to improve sales."

Henry looked into the mirror and pointed to me as I listened to two men deliver a long-winded slide show. "He doesn't look like *he* thinks it's a big meeting. He's just sitting there doodling."

"No," I said, "I'm not—*he's* not—doodling. He's sketching out a better product."

The meeting went on, and the guy who was me offered a few critical comments about the sales numbers. He also made some complaints about the current product in the review session, but during the brainstorming session he didn't share any ideas on how to improve it. In fact, the only thing he did was sit there, apparently frustrated or bored, throughout the meeting.

After work he picked up a few things at the grocery store. When the bagger at the checkout stand smiled, handed him his bags, and said, "Have a good night," he made a half-smile and walked to his car.

When he got home, Mary ran up to him and gave him a loving hug. "Hey, there! How was your day, hon? Did you tell them about your idea?"

"Nah," he replied. "They wouldn't have listened to me anyway. Bunch of morons."

She looked at him sadly and took his coat. He walked to the kitchen and grabbed a beer. Mary followed him in and said, "So you didn't even *tell* them about it? I thought you were really excited about that idea."

"Just let it go, Mary. They'd just shoot it down anyway."

"But—"

"*Let it go, Mary!*" he barked.

He walked into the den, turned on the television, and didn't speak to her the rest of the evening.

The scene looped back to its beginning and froze on the image of me in my bathroom, staring disappointedly at myself in the mirror.

Henry motioned to the image. "Is that who you really are?"

I shook my head sadly. "No."

"Well, then, who is it?"

"I don't know. It's . . . it's not really me."

Henry turned to me. "You know what, sonny? It *is* you. That *was* you we saw, wasn't it? That *was* a real day in your life, wasn't it?"

"Yes," I said. "But it's not the *real* me."

Henry scoffed. "Oh, c'mon! That's a bunch of psychobabble, and you know it. *That* was you. That was *who* you have become. That was who you are now, right?"

I looked at Henry's eyes in surprise. Gone was the cheery cotton-candy man.

He continued. "Hey, listen, sometimes you got to call it like it is. There is no *real* you versus *fake* you. No real self versus false self. You are who you are, wholly and completely. All your emotions and behaviors are a part of who you are now. Unless you accept every aspect of that, you're lying to yourself. You're avoiding yourself. Maybe you don't like parts of who you are, portions of what you just saw, but those are portions and parts of you until you change them. You've got to admit that even the bad parts are parts of you. Otherwise, you'll never change. That *was* you we just saw, right?"

I nodded.

"Then own it. That's how your life is. That's how it's going. That's who you are now. Decide if that's who you really want to be tomorrow."

Henry walked away, leaving me staring at the image in the mirror.

After a few moments I stalked away, disgusted, and started looking for Henry. I passed a few of the mirrors Henry and I had stood in front of earlier. The reflections of me quickly contorted and blurred as I passed. At one mirror, though, I noticed out of the corner of my eye that the reflection wasn't too distorted. I turned and saw a young boy looking back at me. The backdrop behind him was the reflection of the room I was standing in. The boy had long, wavy hair and plump cheeks. He wore a simple white shirt, khaki shorts, white ankle socks, and blue sneakers.

Me when I was six.

Looking at him, I smiled, remembering the innocence of childhood.

He smiled back at me.

I cocked my neck, surprised. He mimicked me. I raised my hand and waved. He waved back.

"I like this game," he said.

Suddenly the background behind him changed. A tall picket fence was a few yards behind him now. And some grass. And a trampoline.

He turned, ran into the yard, climbed onto the trampoline, and started jumping. He giggled and laughed unabashedly. He jumped higher and higher and screeched happily at each new height, "Wheeeee!"

A little girl walked up to the trampoline. It was his neighbor. "Can I jump with you?" she asked.

He stopped jumping. "Yeah. C'mon up."

"I can't get up," she said.

His mother emerged from the back door of the house, but he didn't see her.

"Sure you can," he said, and hopped off. "I'll help you."

He boosted the little girl up; then he taught her how to stagger their jumping so that they could spike each other higher. They laughed and played together for an hour.

Soon the girl's parents called her home and she had to leave. The boy helped her down and said good-bye. "Thanks for jumping with me," he said.

His mom walked over and gave him a tremendous hug, lifting him off the ground and twirling him around. "You're such a good boy!"

"We were jumping," he said.

"I know! I saw you. You were so good!" She put him back onto the trampoline, kicked her shoes off, and climbed up. She grabbed hold of him once more and started jumping with him. "You have such a good heart, my boy. Always make sure you have fun and help others jump higher, and you'll do all right."

I watched them jump together for another ten minutes or so, and I started to tear up. Then the mother said she had to go get dinner ready and got down off the trampoline. Before she turned to go inside, the little boy asked her to wait and started jumping higher and higher. "Look, Mommy, I can go higher than anyone. I can go as high as I want!"

She clapped proudly for him and then went inside.

He played on the trampoline for a few more minutes and then climbed off to go inside. As he walked across the yard he stopped abruptly, as if forgetting something, and headed back toward where I had seen him standing at the beginning of the scene. He looked at me again through the mirror and waved.

I waved back.

Then he took a step through the mirror and stood right in front of me.

"Hi, mister," he said.

My mouth opened, and the tears dropped. "Oh . . . hi . . . hi, little boy."

He looked up at me with bright eyes. "Maybe someday you can come over, and we can jump."

I smiled and tried to hold back the tears. "Sure, sure, you bet we can."

"Okay," he said happily. He stepped forward, hugged my leg, then turned and stepped back into the mirror. He waved at me and started across the lawn.

I reached toward him and hit the surface of the mirror. The image immediately changed, and I stepped back in surprise.

A gunshot.

A slew of sprinters bolted out of their starting blocks.

The scene in the mirror showed me sprinting, coming closer and closer to the finish line, closer and closer to the mirror. I saw myself cross the finish line, and suddenly a seventeen-year-old me stepped out of the mirror. He bent at the waist, trying to catch his breath. He was sweating and wearing a broad smile. He looked up at me.

"That was fast, huh?"

"Fast," I repeated, looking at him with amazement.

He raised his hand, gave me a high-five, and stepped back through the mirror.

The image changed immediately.

The man walked confidently out of his boss's office. It was me again. He shook hands with a longtime co-worker and friend. They had both been given a promotion after a gutsy proposal. He and his friend bumped chests like football players. Then he moved away from his friend and walked through the mirror to stand in front of me. He grabbed me and put me in a headlock and scraped his knuckles across my head. "Smarter than the average bear, ain't we?" he said with a charismatic tone. Then he jumped back into the mirror.

The image changed again.

Mary.

She and the "mirror me" were standing and hugging on the back deck of my new home. A large dinner table, arranged with dozens of candles and roses, stood next to them.

He bent down. "Mary, you've made life worth living, and you have lifted my soul to the stars. Will you share your life with me? Will you marry me?"

Mary lifted her hands to her face in surprise and burst into tears.

"*Oh, my God, yes!*" She pulled him to his feet and kissed him all over his face. He hugged her tightly, rocking her back and forth for what seemed an eternity, not wanting to say a word, not wanting her to hear his voice crack.

Finally, she said, "I'm *so* happy. You make me feel like a princess. I love you so much."

"I just want to be a good man to you, Mary. I want to be a good man."

"You are," she said, nestling into his arms. "*You are . . .* you are . . . you are . . ."

Minutes later she excused herself to wash the mascara from her eyes. As she walked into the house he crashed down into a dinner chair and began crying. Tears of joy fell from his face, and he kept nodding, convincing himself that she had actually said yes.

Then he looked directly at me through the mirror. He nodded approvingly, then whispered, "You *are.*"

PART 3

13
THE LIVESTOCK PAVILION

I walked out of the Hall of Mirrors and took a deep breath. The air felt lighter, crisper. The noise of the people walking by didn't seem so overwhelming. I started down the stairs. Henry was standing to the side, smoking a pipe.

"You smoke?" I asked.

"Nope," he replied, and walked into the crowd.

I laughed and followed. "What do you mean? You're smoking now!"

"You only live once, right?"

Henry's demeanor had changed. He seemed tired, distracted.

We walked south, back toward where the elephants were. We didn't speak. Henry just kept puffing at his pipe and staring off into the distance.

"Is everything okay, Henry?" I asked.

He nodded and took a big draw on his pipe. "Sure, son. I'm just a bit tired. Not as young as I used to be." He smiled at me reassuringly. "But no time for that. We've got a lot of work to do yet."

"What's next?"

"We've got to talk about what you're doing with your life. The scene I saw of you in the Hall of Mirrors wasn't a good thing."

I shook my head and patted his back. "Don't worry about that, Henry. I feel so different now. I'm going to change all that."

Henry stopped and grabbed my shoulder. "I hear you. But let me ask you something. How *long* has that been going on? You disliking your work, arguing with Mary because of it, being stuck in a job and a life that you don't want?"

I thought about it, and my enthusiasm waned. "A few years."

"A few years?"

I looked at the ground. "More than a few."

Henry kicked at the toe of my shoe. "Try about four," he said sternly. "And in the past *four* years, have you ever felt pretty good about yourself, the way you're feeling now, even if just momentarily?"

"Yeah, for a moment here and there, but nothing like this before I . . ."

"Good enough," he continued. "Good enough. But listen, just because you are starting to get over the past and you feel lighter and better because of it doesn't mean you're going to change. We've got to have a serious discussion about why you've allowed all this to go on for four years, because you and I both know the reason isn't just your difficult past—it has to do with the way you've been making your decisions. So, will you agree to talk about all this a little more?"

Henry's voice was hoarse when he spoke. I couldn't tell if it was because of his smoking or if he was just feeling tired or if he was just tired of *me.* Either way, my gut told me something was bothering him.

"Sure, Henry, I'll talk about it."

"Good."

We continued walking south past the animal cages until we came to an enormous steel-sided building.

"The livestock pavilion," Henry said, with a surprising tone of contempt.

"Not a fan?" I asked. "We don't have to go in. I don't like the smell of these places anyway."

"Me neither. But we do have to go in."

We entered the building through a two-story-high garage door. The dirt floor of the pavilion was littered with piles of manure.

Henry crinkled his nose and looked at me. "Yeah. We do have to be in here. The crap that goes on in here has gone on in both our lives. Best we see it so we don't keep stepping in it."

We sat on the top row of the bleachers, four rows above anyone else. We could see the entire pavilion. Metal livestock pens holding cattle, pigs, goats, and horses spread across what must have been two football fields of space. The noise of all the animals was almost deafening. In the middle of the pavilion was a large, fenced-in circle. Henry said that was the exhibition area, where farmers and ranchers showed off their animals.

The place was huge. "I've never seen anything like this before," I said.

"Unfortunately, I've seen a lot of it," Henry said. He spoke in a whisper, almost as if he were talking to himself rather than me.

"Oh?" I asked. "Did you grow up on a ranch?"

"Practically." He looked down into the pens and seemed troubled. "Do you remember . . ." He suddenly erupted in a spasm of coughing. He coughed so hard and for so long that I instinctively reached over and patted him on the back. When he could speak again, he thanked me.

I couldn't help but smirk. "You might want to stay away from that pipe."

"Right," he said, his face turning pale. He spat on the ground and continued. "Do you remember when I vouched for you at the front gate?" he asked.

"Yes, I do. I've been meaning to ask you about it . . . and to thank you for it. I realize that it was, in some way, a big deal. So thank you."

Henry scrutinized me as If checking my sincerity. Then he slapped my knee. "Well, it was my pleasure. I saw something in you. And after seeing Mary's unopened envelope, I knew our stories were *supposed* to overlap. Anyway, if that's the case, I better tell you some of my story." He paused and looked across the pavilion. "Unfortunately, a lot of it happens in places like this." Henry shifted in his seat as if readying himself for a long story. "I suppose my life isn't much different from yours, at least when it comes to the themes that have woven through it. Like you, I thought the world was a dark place for a long time.

"I was raised in Wyoming. Most people don't know that about me. It was cold as hell there, and I don't talk about it much. Just the memories alone sometimes chill me to the bone.

"My dad was a coal miner. He was a big man. Tough and mad at the world because his life hadn't worked out the way he wanted it. But you could tell he loved us. He never said it, but he'd look at us now and then with pride. There was one scene when I was twelve, when he bent down, hugged me hard, looked me straight in the eye—one of the only times I can remember—and said that he *knew* I would make him a proud father. He used to tell all his co-workers that his kids would really make it in the world. He worked and busted his ass and sacrificed his whole life to make sure we could go to school and have a better future than he did.

"Anyway, when I was thirteen, the coal tunnel Dad was working in collapsed. He and twelve other guys were buried alive. . . . They never dug him out."

"Oh, no . . ." The words just fell out of my mouth. "I'm sorry, Henry." I felt partly sorry for him and partly guilty that I had never asked him about his life despite all his questions about my own.

He didn't seem to hear me.

"I remember when Dad went to work that day, down to every detail. He yelled at Will and me—Will was my younger brother—for not doing our chores. Then he said we had to be more responsible and ruffled Will's hair. He said to me, 'Be a good boy. Take care of your brother today. You're bigger than him, Henry, so you should always look out for him and other people.' Before he left he told Mom he'd be home on time like always. He said, 'Thanks for breakfast, darlin'. You're the light that pulls me out of that pit every day.' He always said that to her. Then he was gone.

"Few years later Mom died of a broken heart. Doctors said it was heart failure, a bad valve, but we knew. Will and I didn't have anybody to support us—no family, nothin'. So the local church found us a job and some housing . . . clear across the state. They sent us to work for a rancher named Wade. He agreed to feed us and shelter us. What they didn't know was that he'd work us to the bone and make us sleep in the loft in his barn. Unfortunately, we were too young to make our own decisions; we just went where we were told.

"Wade already had a bunch of ranch hands, and it didn't take Will and me long to figure out we weren't welcome. We were young, weak, and inexperienced. The other hands knew it and reminded us of it every day. They'd give us the chores that no one else wanted, serve us scraps from the lunch table, treat us like dogs any chance they got. If we made a mistake, they wouldn't say a word. Just hit us. With their fists or anything they had in their hands: a rope, reins, a canteen, whatever.

"Poor Will was always so scared, always wettin' his bed, even after he turned fifteen. I always did what I could to protect him. I'd work longer hours so he wouldn't have to. I'd eat less at the lunch table if they underserved us. I'd take the blame for any of his mistakes. I'd raise my hand to volunteer for the tough jobs whenever someone was eyeing him.

"All we ever wanted was to fit in, to be accepted. So we did everything we could to live up to the ranch hands' expectations. We followed their rules. We tried to impress them. We worked harder than anyone would ever expect, hoping for a kernel of recognition.

We'd clean up after them at lunch and dinner. We'd tend to their horses. That was our whole life, trying to become one of them and trying to impress them. But the alienation and abuse continued.

"Will and I talked about leaving all the time. But where would we go? What would we do? We were just two dumb kids. So we stayed. And suffered.

"Then one day, on Will's eighteenth birthday, we decided we were fed up and would leave the next day. We were just going to walk out and venture into the world. We didn't know what we were going to do, but it sure wasn't going to be ranching. That night, to celebrate, I stole a jug of whiskey and got my brother drunk. We talked about all the things we might discover out there in the big world. We drank and danced and sang. At one point, Will was so happy that he spontaneously leaped off the loft into a wagon full of hay below. He did an amazing front flip. He probably wouldn't have done it if I hadn't gotten him drunk."

Henry paused and stared down into the pens.

"Will rotated too far . . . broke his neck on the wagon . . ."

"Oh, no," I said. "Oh, no . . ."

". . . After his death, I just . . ."

Henry seemed to be reliving the scene in his mind. He cleared his throat. "After my brother's death, I left Wade's ranch. I decided to strike out on my own." He shook his head. "You know where I ended up? On another damn ranch! Somehow I'd convinced myself it was all I could do. I only knew one thing: ranching. I let my one talent box me in. Deep skills sometimes mean deep ruts. The pattern continued. I worked my ass off to fit in and impress people. And you know somethin'? At that second ranch it worked. People took notice—so much so that after a year one of the head guys asked me if I wanted to follow him to another ranch for more money. I said, sure, why not? Over the next fifteen years, same thing. I busted my hump to live up to other people's expectations and rules so I could fit in and impress them. Then, whenever someone accepted me, I'd follow them wherever they went. I followed other people's dreams. I went where I knew I might have a chance at belonging and being recognized.

"The tragedy of it all was, I didn't even like ranching! I'd wake up every morning, stare in the mirror, and see a person looking back who was miserable. The eyes always give it away. It was obvious to anyone who looked at me that I was living life at a low level of despair. Eventually I got out, but that's a whole 'nother story." He turned toward me. "But you know why I'm telling you this story? Because I saw *exactly* that same look on your face in the image in the Hall of Mirrors—mildly miserable. Your eyes spoke volumes. You've been living your life at a low level of despair because you're spending your days doing something you honestly could not care less about."

We sat in silence until Henry sat up abruptly and smiled. He pointed down to the exhibition circle.

"You see that calf there? The one standing alone?"

A man on a horse was corralling all the cows and calves to one side of the circle. One calf stood still.

"Yeah. I see him."

"Look at the little guy! Look at his legs."

They were shaking.

"Listen to him."

The calf was making a bawling, helpless noise.

"Look!"

Then the calf trotted clumsily toward the other cows and calves, pushing his way into the middle.

Henry laughed wildly. "Now, that's timing. That's what happens to *us*. We're scared to death to be alone or unattended, so we follow the herd—either doing what we're told or what everyone else is doing."

I got the point but wasn't biting.

"But wait a second," I scoffed. "If that calf didn't stay with the herd, he wouldn't survive."

"Perhaps," Henry said. He turned to me with a grin. "Good thing we're not cows."

We left the pavilion to escape the noise of the animals. When we were a few yards outside the building, Henry asked me to sit on a park bench. "Listen," he said, "you know where I've been going with this. Your career is making you miserable. I have no doubt that you're busy. But you're not fulfilled, and your busy work isn't your life's work. Am I right?"

I stared back into the pavilion. "So this is about getting me to quit my job?"

"No," Henry shot back quickly. "This is about getting you to question *why* you have the job you have. Is your career what you dreamed of, or what you fell into? You and I both know that you haven't stayed in this career because it makes you get up every morning and sing in the shower.

"My guess is, you were like that calf. Someone told you where to go, or you went there so you didn't have to stand alone. I think you were trying to be accepted by someone, so you tried to live up to *their* expectations and impress them by taking that job."

Henry looked at me intently. "Do you know who I'm talking about?"

I looked to the ground and nodded.

"Mary," I whispered.

Henry stood up. "*Now* we're getting somewhere."

14
THE BUMPER BOATS

As we walked from the livestock building back toward the Hall of Mirrors and the merry-go-round, Henry grilled me with questions.

"So you took your job—the one you admittedly don't exactly love—because of Mary?"

"Basically, yeah."

"What do you mean, 'basically'?"

"I mean, she wanted me to have a steady job . . . so we could have a good future together. She was always talking about having a nice home together. So when this job came up, I knew she wanted me to take it."

"Did she tell you that?"

"More or less."

"What do you mean, 'more or less'? Did she say, 'I want you to take that job,' or not?"

"She never verbalized it. She didn't have to."

"So Mary never actually came right out and said she wanted you to take the job?"

"Why are you stuck on that?" I said with some frustration. "No, she didn't exactly *say* it. But again, I knew she wanted me to. Here's the situation: I was laid off from my previous job at the worst possible time. I had just proposed to Mary the month before. And in three weeks I was going to surprise Mary with a trip to the Virgin Islands. Her parents were going to be down there for their thirtieth wedding anniversary. I was going to take her and meet up with them to celebrate our engagement and their anniversary."

Henry sighed. "*Ouch.* That *is* bad timing. So you were laid off? And you canceled the trip?"

"No, I had already. planned and paid for the whole thing, so going was a given. But I'll tell you what, I didn't want to go hang out with her parents as the unemployed fiancé. So I hustled for those three weeks to find another job. By the time we got down there, I had several offers."

"Good for you," Henry said. "That showed some gumption. Were all the offers in the same line of work?"

"No," I said. "Two actually surprised me. They were in public relations, not sales. I had asked my headhunter to see if there were any PR jobs out there, and he found some interest. Anyway, I took the sales gig."

"But you had asked for the PR jobs. Why didn't you take those?"

"Because they didn't pay as much—I just didn't have the skills or experience. And like I said, Mary was always talking about having a house and living the good life together."

"Did you ever talk with Mary about the PR jobs, about what you really wanted to do?"

"No."

"I see," Henry said. "Have you ever wondered what would have happened if you had taken one of the PR jobs?"

"Sure. Every time I'm bored stiff at work. But a man has to make sacrifices to provide for his family."

Henry curled his brow in confusion. "So let me see if I get this right. You assumed what Mary wanted without asking her. You gave up your ambitions and hopes for a more exciting career in order to please her. And in the last four years you've suffered in your job and family because you never spoke up for what *you* really wanted? Is that about right?"

"No. I don't think it is. I think you're putting too much of a bad spin on it. Look, I had just bought a house and I had just got engaged. Sometimes you have to compromise in order to have a good life with someone else. I don't think anyone would disagree with that."

Henry didn't respond.

We came upon a hip-high metal fence that surrounded a giant round pool. Kids were lined up all around the fence, and you could hear them screaming and splashing inside.

Henry smiled. "I love the bumper boats."

We followed the line until we reached the entrance. A short, wavy-haired man stood at the stairway leading up to the deck around the pool. He spotted Henry immediately.

"Henry!" he squealed in a high voice. "Henry! Is that you? I heard you were back—get over here!"

The two men embraced.

"Squirt," Henry called out. "Can you do me a favor?"

"Of course, Henry, what's up?" he replied with enthusiasm.

"I need to go do some detective work about a woman," he said. "Her name is Mary Higgins. You know of her?"

The little guy shrugged. "Never heard of her."

Henry looked at me, then back at Squirt. "Well, could you take care of my friend here for a while? He's been steering his boat by the wrong stars for a while. Actually, he's never really steered it at all. Could you help him out?"

Henry's candid description of me caught me off guard; I felt embarrassment mixed with anger.

"You bet, Henry."

"Thanks, Squirt. See you in a bit."

Henry walked away without saying a word to me. A few yards away he started coughing forcefully again.

~

Squirt and I circled the platform of the pool and watched the kids spin and slam into one another in their bumper boats.

"There are two kinds of kids," Squirt said. He rubbed his chin pensively, as if this had just occurred to him for the first time. "There are the spinners and the sailors. The sailors are the kids who hop into the boat and head for open water—they're the explorers. They have a dream and they set out for it. Yeah, they're dreamers and doers. They know exactly where they want to go. And no matter what bumps into them, they get there, because they keep steering in that direction. They're the ones you'll hear screaming, 'Get out of my way!' The sailors are vocal about what they want. Once they get to the other side, they'll come back and bump everyone. When I blow my whistle letting everyone know time is up, sailors always end up on the other side of the pool from where they started. They gladly hop out of their boats, because they got what they wanted. They got their goal *and* they got to have fun bumping other boats."

Squirt stopped and scanned the pool. He pointed out a little boy spinning in a circle. "Then you've got the spinners. The spinners . . . well, actually, they *start* just like the sailors. They also want to head for open water. But as soon as everyone gets going, the spinners quickly realize there are a lot of other people in the pool. They realize how hard it is to steer. So the spinner does something unique. The spinner makes an assumption: it's hard to steer my boat without bumping into other people, so I won't be able to make it to the other side. Spinners give up quickly. They say, 'Well, I guess I can't make it to the other side, so I'll just have fun here by myself and spin.' They might even bump a few people. They do something that is entirely unhelpful to their original goal, and everyone else's goal: they spin in one place, bumping and blocking everyone from getting to the other side, without even knowing it. Most of the time spinners spin quietly. When I blow the whistle for everyone to stop, they're the last ones to dock, and they're almost always disappointed in their ride."

When he finished speaking, Squirt blew his whistle. The kids started coming in. I noticed how many spinners took longer to come to the platform. Squirt started going from boat to boat, fastening each rope to the dock. Once he did that for each boat, the kid would jump out and head for the exit.

"A little help?" he said, motioning to the boats across the pool.

I walked to the other end and helped kids out of their boats and then tied the boats to the platform.

Squirt and I met back in the middle; then he walked around the platform again, making sure each boat was securely moored.

"You know, my friend," he said condescendingly while walking between two boats, "you are a classic friggin' spinner."

Something about his tone infuriated me. "*What?*" I said. "You don't even know me."

"I know enough. I've heard about you. And I heard what Henry said." He bent down to double-check one of the boats I had moored. "You're a spinner. It's like a billboard on your forehead, buddy."

"Oh, c'mon, that's not fair—you don't know a damn thing about me."

Squirt stood upright. "Yeah? Well, I know a spinner when I see one."

I felt like lashing out with some childish I-know-you-are-but-what-am-I sort of retort. "Listen, I'm not going to argue about—"

"I know you won't argue. That's why you're a spinner, you moron. You don't want to make waves. Now, just admit it—you're a spinner."

"What?"

"Admit it!" he said, stepping toward me. "Right here and now. Admit it!"

"What? This is stupid. I'm not going to—"

Squirt lunged at me. "Spinner!" he cried accusingly.

He grabbed me by the shirt.

We struggled.
We both fell into the pool.
All went black.

I gulped water, panicking and thrashing frantically toward the surface. When I broke through, a bright sun blinded me. I looked around me for Squirt. He was gone. The bumper boats were gone. I felt my feet touch the bottom. I stood and squinted. In front of me lay a sandy beach. The taste of saltwater was in my mouth. *What the ... ?*

I suddenly recognized the beach in front of me: a secluded shore in the Virgin Islands. Where I took Mary to celebrate our engagement.

I heard a familiar laugh ... Mary. Looking up the beach, I could see her walking with her mother, Linda. I waded through the water, staring in confusion. "Mary?" I called out. Neither she nor Linda gave me the slightest notice.

But they were talking about me.

Linda said, "So what is he going to do?"

"I don't know," Mary said. "He told me this morning he had a great job offer as a sales account manager. I guess it's similar to the job he was laid off from, but a move up in pay and prestige. The only thing is, if he takes it, he'd be stuck in an office all day and have to deal with budgetary issues, which he hates. He said it was really good money, though."

"Oh, good," Linda said. She grabbed her daughter's hand and stared happily at the engagement ring. "He's got to start thinking about your future together. I know he just bought a house a while ago, but maybe he'll want a bigger one once you two are married and move in together. Maybe then you'll give me some grandkids?" She smiled. "He should take it. You two need stability and security."

"Yeah," Mary said, staring out into the ocean. "The job definitely pays well. We'd be set. We could have a great house. But no, Mom, no grandkids yet," she said, returning the smile. "We want to wait so we can enjoy our marriage first. You know, do things together. Travel and enjoy life."

Linda said, "Just another reason he should take the job. You two will need money for those travels. Right now you're both barely making it. He's been unemployed for a month. . . . Your job pays okay, but you'll never get rich doing social work. This job sounds like a good thing for both of you. I'm excited to hear about it."

"Yeah, I was really excited too this morning when he told me about it. I was thrilled. He looked so happy about it. He needed that offer, for his own pride." Mary looked off into the bright blue ocean. "I just worry about it."

"Worry about what?" Linda asked.

"I know the money would be good, but I worry he wouldn't like it. I want him to be happy."

"Oh, hon, he's a big boy. He's not going to take a job he doesn't like. He's a smart guy and can do anything he wants. I'm sure he's excited about this job because it'll really set you two up to have a good life together. Like I said: a house, some kids, stability."

"Yeah, but what's all that if he's not happy? I don't want him coming home from work every day miserable like Dad used to. Remember? Remember how miserable Dad was at the bank? Remember how happy he was when he started his own business? I just don't want my husband to ever have to go through that. I don't care if he makes a dollar."

"Honey, I don't think he'd put himself through that," Linda said. "I don't think he'd put *both* of you through that. Besides, you two are good communicators with each other, right? He loves you, and he would talk to you about this more if he were worried about it, right? He's obviously made his decision, and you should support him."

Mary smiled. "I guess you're right. I should be more supportive. He'd tell me if he had doubts."

I stopped walking alongside them and felt as if I were drowning. I looked down and kicked the sand. My heart ached. *Four years wasted. . . .*

When I looked up again, Mary and her mother had disappeared.

I was on the beach alone.

I turned and started walking back down the beach. Then I heard someone in the water calling out to me.

"Honey! Honey! C'mon out and play with me!"

I looked to my left. It was Mary.

"C'mon, honey! Come out here!"

I turned around, expecting to see myself lying on a beach blanket.

"Honey-y-y," Mary pouted, "come play!"

I pointed at myself as if to say, *Are you talking to me?*

Mary laughed. "Yes, you, cutie! C'mere."

Tears formed in my eyes. I walked into the water and waded out to her.

As I got within inches I looked at her as if she were a miracle.

"You . . . you can see me?" I asked.

"Of course," she said, laughing. "Now, come play with me; I'm a damsel in distress."

I reached for her, expecting my arms to pass through her body as if she were a ghost. But they didn't. I felt her. I squeezed her tight and cried uncontrollably. "Honey, oh, how I missed you."

Mary didn't seem to notice that I was crying. She just squeezed me back and giggled playfully. She said, "Remember how much fun we used to have together? Before you took that job? Do you remember how fun life used to be? We always had fun, didn't we?"

"Yeah, honey," I cried. "We always had fun . . . we always did." I squeezed her as hard as I could.

Again Mary laughed as if she hadn't heard me.

"Uh-oh," she cooed as she pulled away and kicked water at me. "I'm drowning. Will you come save me, you big, strong man?"

She smiled and dunked herself under the water.

I laughed and swam toward her. I could see her underwater, smiling up at me.

I took a breath and submerged.

Everything went black again.

15
THE LOOP-DE-LOOP

I awoke lying on my stomach on the deck surrounding the bumper-boat pool. I coughed up some water and rolled onto my back, sucking in air. I was soaking wet and cold. I heard the muffled sounds of men arguing. I shook the water out of my ears.

Across the pool, Squirt and a tall man with big arms and a bulging belly were screaming at each other. Squirt's clothes were still dripping. The big guy hollered and pointed furiously to the exit steps. Squirt bowed his head and walked down them. A few seconds later a wave of kids came up onto the platform and hopped into the boats.

They looked at me angrily, as if I had delayed their ride.

The tall man walked toward me so fast that the tools hanging from his tool belt clanged together. I tried to get up, but my body felt exhausted.

He knelt beside me. "You okay?"

"Yeah. What happened?"

The man pursed his lips and glared at Squirt, who was now on the other side of the pool, unmooring the boats. "Ah, you were just a victim of Squirt's short-man complex. Let's get you up and get you dried off before you catch cold."

He offered his hand to help me up. I looked at him hesitantly.

"It's okay. You can trust me. Henry asked me to meet up with you. They call me Crank." He offered his hand again, and I noticed the grease under his fingernails.

He helped me to my feet. I felt dizzy and had to put my arm around him to keep from falling back to the ground.

"Go ahead, lean on me," he said.

We walked slowly to the exit and started down the stairs.

"Hey, Spinner!" Squirt called from behind me.

I turned, and Squirt threw me a towel. "Now you know what I was sayin'. You gave up on doing what you wanted because you assumed there would be too many waves. Then you sat spinning and blocked both you and Mary from your goal: a good life together." He smiled smugly, then turned and untied another boat.

Crank and I sat at the base of the Cyclone. The carts roared past, circling the single-loop track over and over again. The circular metal frame of the ride vibrated and rattled noisily.

"I've been maintaining this ride for a long time," Crank said, gazing at the speeding carts. "I've never understood why people love it so much. They get in the coaster carts, and the carts back halfway up the circle, fall forward, and make it halfway up the other side, fall backwards with more momentum up the other side, then fall forward again, this time with just enough momentum to make it to the top of the loop. The carts sit at the top for a few seconds, then fall back down the loop, then up, then over the hump, then back down. The cycle continues over and over again until people feel numb or queasy. They just can't get enough of it. . . . I don't get it."

We watched in silence until the ride came to an end.

Crank stood up. "Maybe you can explain it to me."

He hopped off the base of the ride and walked over to the operator. He pointed at me and then at the ride. The operator pointed to the line of kids waiting their turn. They spoke a minute more, and the operator nodded. Then he turned to the kids waiting in line and said something. They booed him as he hung a sign: RIDE TEMPORARILY CLOSED FOR MAINTENANCE.

Crank walked back toward me with a grin.

"What's going on?" I asked.

"Are your clothes still wet?" he asked.

"Yeah."

His grin widened. "Get ready to be blow-dried."

I climbed into the front cart, and Crank lowered the safety bar and cage over me.

"Now, I just want you to enjoy the ride. No tricks here. You'll get dry, and I'll get my information. Pay attention to what you feel. I want you to describe it to me later. Ready?"

"Yeah."

Crank turned toward the operator and waved his hand in a circle. "Giddyap!" he said.

The operator pushed a button, and I heard a buzzing noise below. The ride started backing up, and I sensed the carts behind me climbing up the right side of the loop. I had just begun to feel the pull of gravity when there was another buzz; then the carts plummeted forward. I went back and forth several more times until I was poised about halfway up the right side of the loop, looking down toward its base. The carts let loose, and I felt the wind rush in my face. The ride surged upward and slowed just as it reached the top of the loop. I was upside down, weightless, the safety bar holding me in place. Blood rushed to my head. Then the ride dropped down the other side, then back up, then over the hump, where I was upside down, then back down the other side. The first few loops made me feel energized as I felt the pull of gravity and the fear of falling and the wind against my face and the surge of momentum. The ride went on for several minutes. Up one side, over the hump upside down, then back down the other side. Up, over, down. Up, over, down. Then suddenly, the energy turned into numbness. Then queasiness. Then numbness again. Up, over, down.

Finally, the ride slowed, and I heard the sound of brakes. The ride was over.

Crank lifted the safety cage. I could barely stand. He chuckled and helped me out.

For several minutes I paced back and forth across the walkway from the ride, just trying to get my bearings back. Crank walked with me, saying nothing but chuckling to himself every time the ride looped and the kids on board squealed with delight. He kept looking at me expectantly.

"I don't know what to tell you, Crank," I said. "Why *do* people like that ride? I don't know—I hated it."

He let out a hearty laugh. "Me too! Why'd you hate it?"

I told him about the numbness and queasiness.

"Yeah. That'll make for a miserable experience." He paused and motioned for us to sit on a nearby bench. When we sat, he looked at me in a way that said it was time to get serious. "Shouldn't be a big problem for you, though. Henry said you were used to being on a miserable ride."

I pretended I hadn't heard the comment. "So . . . where is Henry?"

Crank watched the carts loop around the top. "He's looking into some things. Handling some business. Shouldn't be long." He gave me a reassuring look. "Henry told me about you and updated me on your situation. Thought it would be good for us to talk."

I felt embarrassment. "What did he tell you about me?"

Crank shrugged. "Everything. Nothing. Enough so that I might be able to help you. I'm pretty good in these matters."

"What matters?"

"The matters you're facing. The reason you're so off track in life right now."

"What reason is that?"

Crank pointed to the Cyclone. "You're stuck in a negative cycle. You haven't been able to break free. It's making you numb and queasy."

I blinked in confusion. "I'm sorry, I'm not following. What are we talking about here? What cycle?"

Crank looked at me as if I should know. "The cycle of silence."

"Silence?" I asked.

"That's it." Crank nodded authoritatively. "The cycle of silence. It has more to do with your present than your past, that's for sure. *Silence.* It's a cycle, a patterned behavior . . . a loop-de-loop of suffering. And you're stuck in it, bad. Since I'm the mechanic for this ride," he said, motioning to the carts whirring around the loop, "Henry thought I could help you. Is it okay if we talk?"

I nodded.

"You know, there are a lot of ways to explain this to you. I'm not as good as Henry or some of the other guides you've met, so you'll have to forgive me."

"Other guides?"

Crank looked at me again as if I should understand what he was saying. "Yeah, the other guides. The people you've met here in the park. The wizard, Harsh, Gus, Willie, Squirt, me. We all have something to teach; we're all here to help. It might not always seem that way," he said, nodding toward the bumper boats, "but we're here to help."

I looked at the bumper-boat pool. "Yeah. Squirt wasn't exactly the counselor type."

Crank frowned. "I know. Believe me, I gave him hell for what he did. See, we can all teach you in any way we think will be effective. A lot of these new guys are rough, though. Henry is going to be pissed. There's just two rules we don't break, and Squirt took it too far."

"Two rules?" I asked.

"We don't kill you, and we don't kill love in your life. That's it. Squirt nearly drowned you to get a point across. Henry will think he went too far. I guess Henry and I are from simpler times. We'd both rather talk it through."

Crank shook his head as if he had revealed too much. "Back to you. Let's talk about your cycle and how to break it. Do you know what I mean when I talk about the cycle of silence?"

I thought about Mary and Linda talking on the beach. "You mean that I didn't talk to Mary about my doubts?"

"That's an example. But it goes beyond that. Let me ask you some quick questions. Did you ever tell anyone about your dad hitting you?"

A dark feeling stirred in my gut. "No."

"Did you ever talk to anyone about your grandpa's death?"

"Uh, no."

"Did you ever talk to anyone about being laid off?"

"Not really."

"Did you ever express your doubts to Mary about taking the new job?"

"No."

"Did you ever tell your co-workers at your new job about your innovative product ideas?"

"No."

"Did you ever talk to anyone about Mary's leaving?"

I shook my head.

"Well, now you have a better idea of what I'm talking about. It's a cycle of silence. You've lived your whole life holding in your feelings, your thoughts, your concerns, your dreams, your nightmares. You're looping the same old story: 'I don't want to impose my world on anyone. . . . I don't want to be a pest.'

"Here's the truth. If you stay in this cycle, if you don't start telling the world how you feel and what you want, then you'll be forever stuck on the same life track you're on now—a track that makes you feel numb and queasy. And the only way to break the cycle is to understand how it began in the first place and then slow it down and stop it."

"I'm not sure I know how to do that."

Crank smiled. "That's why I'm here. I'm the mechanic. I'm here to get you on track. Let me talk shop with you for a second, and I think I can help you. You remember the ride?" he said, pointing again to the Cyclone. "Well, let me tell you how it works. It's all about momentum. A jolt of energy gets the carts moving—that's the buzzing you heard—then momentum takes it from there. The carts go around the track because of bursts of energy, momentum, and the path of least resistance. You get something moving on the path of least resistance, and it will go forever."

Crank looked at me intently. "Do you know what the energy source was that started your cycle of silence?"

"My dad."

"The abuse?" he asked.

"Yeah."

"Okay. Well, whatever might have started it isn't important. And you know from your earlier experiences here at the park that you can't blame your dad for the momentum you've picked up on this cycle. You've chosen not to express yourself. You've chosen to remain silent. You've chosen the path of least resistance. Do you agree?"

"I guess."

"No guessing here," Crank said firmly. "In life, the path of least resistance is always silence. If you don't express your feelings and thoughts to others, you don't have to deal with their reactions to it. You don't have to feel vulnerable. You don't risk rejection. But I'll tell you what: the path of least resistance leads exactly where that ride leads to." He pointed again to the carts looping around the track. "Nowhere."

He grabbed my shoulder and kept pointing at the carts whirring around the circle. "Let me ask you something. Aren't you *tired* of that ride? Aren't you *tired* of feeling numb and queasy?"

"I am."

"Then you've got to stop the cycle. You can't keep giving this behavior energy. You've got to *refuse* the path of least resistance. You've got to put the brakes on this behavior, or your same story of suffering will just keep looping over and over. It's time you start expressing how you feel and what you want. That will start a new cycle for you. And you can't just express yourself now and then. You've got to do it from now on. You've got to start building momentum—then you'll be unstoppable. Just break the cycle of silence and suffering. Start a new cycle of strength by expressing to the world how you feel and what you want. It's the only way you'll ever live the life you want. Got it?"

"But what if I don't know what I want?"

Crank stood. "Well, then, ever wonder what you're going to get?"

16
THE FORTUNE-TELLER

Crank led me past the bumper boats and back toward the animal cages and the Big Tent. I noticed that the crowds of people were thinning. "Where is everyone?" I asked him.

He motioned toward the Big Tent. "The night's main attraction starts in about two hours. They're probably up on the midway getting some food. They'll want to be early in line for the big show."

As we neared the animal cages, I saw Henry talking with Gus.

"Hey, Henry!" I said from afar. I felt a sense of comfort in seeing him again.

Henry nodded, turned to Gus, and gave him a hug, then approached us with a smile.

"How are you?" he asked me warmly.

I almost couldn't answer. Henry's face was paler than before. His eyes were still vibrant, but he looked exhausted.

"I'm . . . I'm good, Henry. How about you? You don't look so good."

Henry beamed a wide smile. "Well that's a lovely thing to say!" He chuckled, then coughed. "I'm good. Don't worry about this old man. Crank, where were you headed?"

Crank replied, "I was taking him to see Meg."

"Oh, Meg!" Henry said, looking at Crank with surprise. "Well, I hope she behaves. You know how she can be."

He turned to me. "Listen, after you see Meg, meet me over at the entrance to the Big Tent, okay?"

"Sure. Who's Meg? Where are you going?"

"You'll meet Meg soon enough. I'm off to handle a few things. You go ahead now. See you at the Big Tent."

Crank and I walked past the animal cages and turned left. The back of the Big Tent was now on our left, and a long row of smaller tents stood on our right. Crank guided me to a tent in the middle of the row where a make-shift sign hung outside: KNOW YOUR FUTURE NOW, $1.

"Not a bad deal," I said, chuckling.

"Glad you think so."

Crank glanced over his shoulder toward the back of the Big Tent. "Remember to meet Henry on the other side once you're done. Don't stray. It was a pleasure meeting you."

"Thanks, Crank. You too. I really appreciate what you told me."

"Good. Take care." He motioned for me to enter the small tent, then walked back toward the animal cages.

———

Inside the tent the air was heavy with incense. A half-dozen lit candles sat on a small black coffee table directly in front of me. Next to the table stood a single chair, and a few feet past it hung a heavy red velvet curtain.

"Sit down," a frail voice called from behind the curtain. "I'll be with you shortly."

I sat. A few minutes passed; I heard weeping.

The curtain opened, and Harsh the Hypnotist emerged. He stared at me in surprise, then fixed me with an ominous look. He walked to the tent exit. "You better be worth it, kid."

As the tent flap closed behind him the voice behind the curtain called again. "Come on in. We haven't got all night."

Pushing back the curtain, I saw a woman wrapped in a tattered purple robe, sitting behind a small round table. Her face was leathery with age; her gray hair was wrapped in a faded red bandanna, and silver hoop earrings hung from her ears. On the center of the table in front of her sat a crystal ball. A haze of incense smoke lingered above us.

"Slt," she said, looking me up and down. "I'm Meg. And you're the one causing all the talk."

"All the talk?" I repeated.

She looked at me expectantly and held out her hand. "Sorry, this old gal only barks for a buck."

"Oh," I said, embarrassed. I fished in my pocket for a dollar. "Here you go."

She snatched the dollar from my hand and put it in a little pouch hanging from her neck. Satisfied, she said, "Now, what do you want to know?"

"You said I'm the one 'causing all the talk.' What talk is that?"

"I'm a fortune-teller, not a gossip," she said, suddenly testy. She stood up and relit an incense stick.

"Okay," I said, confused. "So what are we supposed to do here? Look into the crystal ball and see my future?"

"No," she scoffed. "You watch too many movies."

She sat back down and pointed toward the crystal ball. "I got that dumb thing for two dollars at the flea market. It's a fishbowl turned upside down."

She saw the look on my face and broke into laughter. "Boy, you're just like Harsh— way too serious!"

I remembered what I'd heard in the waiting area. "Harsh . . . I heard him crying while I was waiting. I guess he must have found out some bad news, huh?"

"He sure did," she said flatly.

I cocked my head. "Well, can I ask what the bad news was? Or would that be gossiping?"

"Of course you can ask. It has to do with your future. Harsh was asking about it."

"Harsh was asking about my future?" I asked. "Why?"

"He was wondering if you would change in the future. He said you were full of excuses. He was worried you wouldn't."

The image of Harsh towering over me flashed in my mind, and I felt a flare of anger. "What does he care whether or not I change?"

"Oh!" Meg said, raising her hands to her cheeks and feigning surprise at my anger. "Don't get so worked up, dearie. I don't think he really *does* care about you that much. He cares about Henry, though—that's why he was weeping."

"The bad news was about Henry?"

"Yes. About Henry . . . and you."

"Bad news about both of us? What is it?"

Meg leaned forward and put her elbows on the table, then said matter-of-factly, "The bad news for both of you is that you don't change."

"What? I don't change?" I thought about all that had happened to me in the park so far. "I don't believe it."

Meg looked at me dispassionately. "It doesn't matter whether you believe it. It is so. And that's bad news for both of you. That's why Harsh was weeping: because he heard the bad news about Henry."

"I don't understand. Why is it bad news for Henry?"

"Because, of course, Henry wants to see you change. He sacrificed to get you in and wants to see you succeed."

"What do you mean, 'he sacrificed'? What sacrifice?"

"I'm afraid that's not for me to say. Henry will tell you in time, I imagine. Unless Harsh tells him the bad news first."

I looked at her in disbelief. "What do you mean, 'not changing'? Listen, lady, you got it wrong. I *have* changed already. I *am* changing my life the second I get home—you don't have to worry about that. Neither does Henry."

Meg raised an eyebrow and nodded as if impressed. "Oh, good for you, dear." Then she sat silently and just stared at me.

An awkward few moments passed.

"So," I said, feeling a bit rattled, "you don't think I change?"

"I know you don't," she said.

"How do you know? Why don't I change?"

"Let me see your hands," she said.

She examined my palms closely for several moments, then looked up at me sadly and squeezed my hands. "Yep, I was right—bad news."

"What? What can you tell from my hands? What can you see?"

"See for yourself," she said, and slapped my hands onto the crystal ball.

A searing bolt of electricity shot through my body. My eyes felt as if they were on fire, and the hair on my neck stood up. I felt my muscles spasm as a deafening roar filled my ears.

A vast white space filled my vision, and suddenly I seemed to be falling at a tremendous speed. The space changed colors: green . . . falling faster . . . yellow . . . faster . . . orange . . . faster . . . black . . . a sudden stop.

A flash of white.

My body feels as if it is floating. I open my eyes. I'm in a church. I can see everything around me. I sense that I'm hovering over the parish, but I have no sense of my physical body. I see a handful of people crying, then a man speaking behind the altar. Then I see myself—lying in a casket.

Another bolt of electricity.

Hovering above my office now, I see myself sitting and staring numbly out the window. I'm older; my sideburns are graying. Wrinkles line my face. The scene fast-forwards, and I walk down the hall past co-workers without saying a word. I go to meetings about things I don't care about. . . . I answer e-mails . . . drive home . . . watch TV . . . drink beer. I'm alone.

Another surge.

I'm back in the church, hovering above the pews, looking down at myself in the casket. At the altar, a stranger stands behind the podium. "He was a good man. I recently just met him. He'd worked at our company for thirty-five years. He was loyal and he kept to himself, but those who knew him seemed to like him." A church woman sitting a few rows back whispers to another, "Poor man died alone." The pastor stands behind the podium. "Would anyone like to say a few words?" No one rises.

My eyes start burning, and scenes from my life flash by: a gasping last breath in bed . . . a Christmas by myself . . . a bland day at work . . . a night at a hospital bed with Mary . . . a night on my porch . . . a horse ride in an open field . . . an aquarium full of clothes hangers.

Zap!—I'm hovering in a room. Mary stands silently. I see myself standing not far away in the kitchen. Mary has tears in her eyes. She looks at me seriously. She is saying, "I think I need to go away for the weekend. I was going to ask you to come with me, but I don't think you're ready."

I hear myself ask a question, but I can see only her face. "Where are you going? I'm not ready for what?"

She says, "You're not ready for change," and walks out the door.

I feel myself screaming, "*Nooo!*"

My hands burn . . . another bolt of electricity . . . a fantastic flash of white.

I felt myself slam into the back of my chair.

I opened my eyes to see Meg, sitting impassively across the little round table. The crystal ball was glowing a deep bluish-purple.

"Jesus!" I screamed out, waving my hands frantically in the air, trying to cool them.

"No, just Meg," she said matter-of-factly and stood up. "I'll be back in a few minutes." She pushed aside the red velvet curtain behind me and walked out.

By the time Meg came back, my hands felt numb, as if I had dipped them in snow and then entered a warm room.

"I don't believe it," I said emphatically as she sat back down. "I won't let my life turn out like that. I don't believe what I saw."

She shook her head. "You're just like Mary—you don't believe what you see with your own soul."

"What?" I said in surprise. "Mary? You met Mary?"

"Of course."

My heart jumped. "Here?"

Meg parted her lips and furrowed her brow as if to say, *Yeah, what are you, stupid?*

"What happened? Why was she here? What did you say to her? Do you know what happened to her?" The questions spilled out so fast that they blurred together.

Meg looked at me vacantly. "She was here for the same reason as Harsh. She wanted to know if you would change. She discovered the answer was no."

"But it's not!" Pain and anger and hurt clenched in the pit of my stomach. "How could you say that? I *will* change! How could you tell her I wouldn't! What did she say?"

"I didn't tell her anything," Meg said. "Mary saw what she needed to see. Then she asked if she should leave you."

"If she should *leave* me? What did you say?"

Meg looked at me coldly. "I told her yes."

"What! How could you! Who do you think you are?" I stood up as if I were about to charge out.

Meg stood and pointed to my seat. "*Sit down!*" she commanded. Her voice seemed to bounce through every cell of my body.

I crumpled into my chair, on the verge of tears. I could barely breathe. The room felt like a coffin; the world felt as if it had collapsed on me.

"*Why?*" I blurted through my hands covering my face. "Why did you tell her that? Don't you know how badly that must have hurt her? I could have changed! Why don't you believe I could have changed?"

Meg whispered her response: "Because you don't know what you want in life. If you don't know what you want, you can't change from here to get there. You have nothing to reach for, nothing to measure yourself against. It doesn't matter if you've sword-fought with dear old Dad, or ridden horses with Grandma, or swum in the crystal blue ocean with Mary. Just because you feel better about the past and who you are doesn't mean your life will change. This is now. In here, we talk about the future. You have to know where you want to go and adjust your course . . . or you just drift."

Meg paused until I looked at her. Her eyes were compassionate. "I told Mary you were a drifter and always would be."

My heart broke. Anger seared the back of my throat. I opened my mouth to let the feeling erupt. No words came out.

"I'm sorry," Meg said. "But if you don't decide what you want in life, you can't change your course to get it. No goals, no growth. No clarity, no change. I'm sorry."

She extinguished an incense candle, patted my shoulder, and walked out of the room once again.

PART 4

17
THE TIGHTROPE

I sat motionless in Meg's tent for nearly an hour. My mind replayed everything she had told me and everything I had seen in the crystal ball. I began to realize that I had spent much of my life frozen in the past or paralyzed in the present. I had never really looked at things long-term. I had never thought about the last days of my life and who I wanted to be or what I wanted to have accomplished. Mary's and Meg's words echoed over and over: *"You're not ready for change"* . . . *"No clarity, no change"* . . . *"You're a drifter."* Meg's words still angered me, yet my heart filled with grief at the thought of Mary sitting in this very chair and seeing the future, a future in which I would never change. I imagined the pain she must have felt, the disappointment, the frustration, the hopelessness—the same feelings I felt when I hovered above my life and saw how it turned out.

Eventually, sadness turned to stillness. I wasn't sure how to interpret what Meg had said or what she had shown me, but I was going to do something about it. I looked at the crystal ball and decided to defy the verdict. *I will not end up that way.* I reached up and smacked the crystal ball off the table. It hit the wall and fell to the floor with a hollow *clunk.* I picked it up. I couldn't believe it—it was plastic. Meg was telling the truth. It really was a cheap fishbowl turned upside down. I turned it over and over in my hands.

The red velvet curtain behind me opened, and Henry emerged. He stared at me and at Meg's vacant chair. "What's going on here? Is everything okay? Where's Meg?" His complexion still looked pale, amplified even more by his concern.

"She left," I said.

Henry frowned. "What do you mean, 'she left'?"

"She just got up and left."

Henry scratched his head. "Why would she . . . well, are you okay?"

"Yeah. I'm . . . fine, I think. . . . I have a new perspective."

"Great! Then Meg was good to you?"

I took a moment to think about his question. "No, Henry, she wasn't. She showed me some things that truly broke my heart. I'm not sure exactly what to think. Maybe I needed to see those things to change? I just don't know. I'm confused. But I'll tell you what: I won't let my life end up that way."

Henry stared again at her empty chair, looking lost in thought. "I just can't understand that woman. She knows not to leave anyone alone." He shook his head and looked back at me. "Let's talk about it on the way?"

"On the way?" I asked.

"To the show. Remember? You were supposed to meet me at the Big Tent."

The Big Tent's entrance was packed with throngs of eager fairgoers. Everyone was milling about, chatting, eating, waiting for the tent to open so they could get good seats.

The excitement in the air only amplified my energy in telling Henry about my future, about how damn sure I was that I wouldn't let my life turn out the way Meg had predicted. The ideas and hopes and dreams about my new life gushed out of me faster than I could process them. I told him about how I would apply all that I had learned at the park. I promised never to live in the past again or get bogged down working on things I wasn't passionate about. I told him I would never end up lonely at the end of my life. I spoke of love and passion and family and faith. I don't know if I was reacting to Meg or summoning old ambitions, but I swore to start over and make my life count.

At some point I began to feel like a kid in a toy store speaking to the deaf ears of a parent. Henry was listening, but he was distracted. He struggled to lead me through the crowd of people to the front of the tent. At the entrance stood two large men in blue shirts with yellow lettering: SECURITY. Both men smiled at the sight of Henry, and one of them pulled back the enormous tent flap for us. The crowd screamed with excitement. The other security guard waved and crossed his arms and called out, "No, not yet, folks!

Not yet!" The crowd booed as Henry and I hurried inside.

"Henry," I said, sounding like a wheedling child, "have you even been listening to what I've been saying? I'm going to *change.*" I looked at him, expecting encouragement.

But he just nodded and said, "I'm happy you're excited to change. But let me ask you something I asked you earlier. Have you ever been excited to change your life before and not done it?"

I felt the wind go out of my sails. "Yes, but, Henry, this is different. I . . ."

"I know, it's different," he interrupted. "I know you're excited about all this, and I couldn't be more thrilled that you want to change. But I know you've dreamed before and let those dreams die in the daylight. You've hoped before, but didn't hop out of bed In the morning to make those hopes reality. I am excited for you, and I don't mean to disparage your good intentions. But I know you have more to learn before you'll ever change. That's why we're here—I want you to learn from the best. C'mon."

He led me down the entrance aisle, which was at least twelve feet wide and bordered by two double-high sections of bleachers. At the end of the aisle I could see the true immensity of the tent. Bleachers lined the high canvas walls, and in the middle of them was a circular open area the diameter of a football field, containing three huge, intersecting red rings about two feet high. The middle ring was a quarter again the size of its neighbors. A couple of dozen men were securing sections of a large cage in the ring to the left. High above the rings, a spiderweb of wires connected dozens of tall metal towers, making up the structure of the tent. The massive framework of a lighting system hung from the wires just above the left and right rings, so that the entire space had the feel of a state-of-the-art concert arena.

"Nice, huh?" Henry said.

We walked about a third of the way around the rings, then up an aisle between two sets of bleachers. At the aisle's end two more security guards greeted us. One shook Henry's hand. The other smiled at me and pulled back the flap.

Just as he spoke, both the guards' radios squawked, "Get ready! We're about to let 'em in!" We all turned and looked toward the entryway, where a sea of people began flooding in.

The guard pulling back the flap looked at me, then at Henry. "Henry, you better get situated."

Henry nodded and ushered me through the flap.

The other side was a scene of chaos. Performers were readying themselves frantically: half-dressed clowns, scurrying trapeze artists, and assistants running everywhere, putting makeup on the performers or helping them step into their costumes. All were hurrying and crying out for more help.

"It's always crazy before the show," Henry said.

"I guess," I muttered.

Henry led me past a long bank of mirrors bordered by enormous lightbulbs. Stopping at the first empty stool in front of the mirrors, he said, "Sit tight. I'll be right back."

I sat watching the performers get ready for about twenty minutes. Then a gigantic roar came from the other side of the flap. I could hear a muffled announcement.

"We're on!" yelled a clown, and a dozen of them filed through the flap. The crowd rumbled and laughed and clapped.

Ten minutes passed, and there came another inaudible announcement, at which point a group of what appeared to be gymnasts disappeared through the flap. More rumblings from the crowd.

Ten more minutes passed, with sporadic loud applause. More announcements, and four women with dozens of silver hula hoops around their necks hurried out.

~

That's him over there!"

I looked up to see a woman in a sequined leotard pointing me out to a man in white stretch pants and a tight sequined shirt. The man walked over to me and introduced himself with a deep Italian accent. "I am Berto Zanzinni."

I shook his hand and looked at him as if to say, *Okay, nice to meet you. Why are you talking to me?*

Berto frowned. "You don't know who I am?"

"Sorry, no. I'm just waiting here for my friend Henry."

"Yes. I know. Henry sent me. I am Berto." He looked at me as if I should know who he was. "Berto," he repeated with a tinge of frustration, "Berto Zanzinni. Of the world-famous

Flying Zanzinnis." He grinned at me as if I should now drop to one knee before royalty.

I looked at him blankly.

"Henry did not tell you we would be meeting?"

"No, he didn't."

Berto laughed and smacked my shoulder. He called over the woman who had pointed me out earlier. "Luisa, come over here, love—you will love this. Grab Antonelli too!"

Luisa disappeared behind a curtain and emerged with a man whom I guessed was Antonelli. She walked up and hugged Berto. Antonelli stood next to them, looking me up and down.

"Luisa, Antonelli, our volunteer here does not know he's a volunteer. Henry told him nothing."

"Didn't tell him *anything?!*" Luisa said, her beautiful olive face aglow. "Nothing! Oh, Berto! We are going to have fun tonight, no?" She laughed giddily.

Antonelli didn't say a word.

I looked at them, frightened. "Henry didn't tell me what? What do you mean, 'volunteer'? What's going—"

Berto interrupted. "What is your pant size, man?"

"What?"

"Your pant size? What is it? Thirty-six waist, thirty-two long? You are about a hundred seventy-five pounds, yes, no?"

"Yes, about that. Why?"

Berto and Antonelli turned and walked away.

Luisa smiled at me. "Because we need to get you dressed and ready, silly."

"Ready for what?" I asked, terrified that I already knew the answer.

"To perform! To walk on air with the world-famous Zanzinnis!" she sang and walked away.

⁓

Drop your pants!" Luisa commanded. She grinned, handed me a sequined shirt and a pair of white tights, and pushed me behind a curtain.

I stood in the dressing area, frozen in terror. What was Henry *thinking?*

"Hurry!" Luisa called.

I squeezed into the outfit and looked in the mirror. I looked pathetic—too big and clumsy for the outfit.

The curtain parted, and Antonelli grabbed me by the arm. "C'mon, we're on!"

We trooped out of the performers' area and up the aisle between the bleachers.

I stopped at the end of the aisle, in awe. Every seat in the tent was filled.

Antonelli pulled me toward the center ring. Someone grabbed my arm. It was Henry. "Do what they tell you," he said, pulling me close. "You want to prove to yourself and to me that you're ready for change? Then do what they tell you."

I looked at him in horror.

Antonelli pulled me away.

"And have fun!" Henry hooted after us.

A spotlight beam landed on Berto and Luisa, who were in front of us. Then another lit Antonelli and me.

In the middle of the ring, the ringmaster, dressed in white tights, a red overcoat with gold buttons, and a black top hat and cane, crowed with delight. "And here they are, folks, the world-famous Flying Zanzinnis!"

The crowd erupted in wild applause as Berto and Luisa walked up to the ringmaster.

Antonelli walked me over to the base of a tall metal tower just outside the center ring. "Get ready to smile," he said.

Berto grabbed the ringmaster's microphone. "Ladies and gentlemen, tonight you will see us fly!"

The crowd applauded excitedly again.

"We will perform several death-defying acts on the trapeze and high-wire. And just for you, just for tonight, we have a special surprise. Here is my beautiful sister to tell you about it!"

He handed Luisa the mike. "Yes, ladies and gentlemen, we have a truly special surprise! Tonight we have chosen a member of the audience to help us kick off the show! This person from the audience, a person just like you, will make his first-ever high-wire walk! Please welcome the newly joined member of our family, our new adopted brother, the *fourth* Zanzinni!"

Luisa pointed to me, and a spotlight beam lit my face once again.

More eager applause.

"Up!" Antonelli commanded.

I looked to the top of the tower. "I can't!"

"No choice now!" he screamed and lifted me up onto the first rung of the tower. He pushed my behind with his palms. "Up!"

I looked at him hesitantly. The crowd picked up on my reluctance and started clapping. "Up! Up! Up!" they chanted.

I climbed up a few rungs on the tower, and the crowd went nuts.

As we climbed higher, Antonelli barked out commands. "When you get to the platform at the top, stand to the side so I can join you. I will teach you to walk the wire. Do not be afraid. I will be holding your hands the entire time. There is a net below. You are totally safe. I will not let you get hurt. Just do as I say, when I say it."

I stood on top of a two-foot-square platform more than sixty feet off the ground. There was nothing to hold on to except a half-inch cable that ran from the platform to the top of the tent. My palms were pouring sweat. I looked down; I didn't see any net. My legs were shaking so violently that I thought I might fall off before I ever started. My heart felt as if it were going to jump out of my chest and climb back down.

Antonelli climbed onto the platform and grabbed hold of the same wire I was holding. He stood between me and the ledge of the platform.

"Look at me!" he barked and pointed to his eyes. "Look!"

Panicked, I stared into his eyes.

"Listen to me! Drown out the sound of the crowd. Just look at me. Just listen. This is your moment of truth. You see Luisa on the platform across from us? Just look over my head—you're taller than me. Do you see Luisa?"

A wire ran from the base of the platform we were standing on to another platform about forty feet away, where Luisa stood smiling at me.

My voice trembled. "I see her."

"Good," Antonelli said. "Now, I want you to focus on her. Our goal is to reach her. *Your* goal is to reach her. To get there you have to block out all the noise you hear except my voice. You need to block out all the feeling in your body except absolute resolve to reach the other side. Do you understand me so far?"

I nodded hesitantly.

Antonelli smiled. "Okay. You're doing fine. Just keep looking at Luisa. Pretend that if you do not reach her, she will be killed."

I stared at Luisa and tried to drum up courage. I could see Antonelli in my peripheral vision, bending and reaching for something under the platform. When he stood, he was holding a long white staff that looked like a broomstick, only longer.

"Look at me again," he said firmly. "Now, listen. Here's what we're going to do. I'm going to walk out on this wire backward. I'm going to be holding this staff parallel to the ground out in front of me. All you're going to do is follow me onto the wire. You're going to be able to balance by holding on to the staff. Get it? Just follow me onto the wire and hold on to the staff. Then I'll walk backward. You walk forward. Get it?"

I shook my head—not because I didn't understand, but because I didn't want to do it.

Antonelli turned and waved toward Luisa, who slowly took a few steps out onto the wire . . . then a few more. Then a few more, until she was about half of the way across. Then she knelt down and held on to the wire with her hands.

"Look," Antonelli said, "you have to go out. *We* have to go. Luisa can't hang out there by herself for very long. We need to reach her before she can go back to the platform. You hear me? We have to go. All you have to do is put one foot in front of the other. Just look at Luisa over my shoulder as we walk and use the staff I'll be holding out for balance. You don't even have to look down. Just put one foot in front of the other slowly, feeling the wire below your foot before putting your weight on it. Don't look down. Just look at Luisa. Your goal is to reach her. Here we go."

Antonelli stepped backward onto the wire. The crowd gasped. He raised the staff in front of him parallel to the ground.

"Put both your hands on the staff," he commanded.

I reached out and grabbed the pole.

Antonelli said, "Great job. You're doing fantastic. Keep your eyes on Luisa. Now, just put one foot out in front of you and onto the wire. Feel the wire below your foot before you put your weight onto it."

Fear shot through my body. I looked into Antonelli's eyes. "I can't! I can't do it!"

Antonelli looked at me calmly. "You must. This is what it's all about. Don't let Meg be right. To change, you must move forward. This is your chance. The life you want is on the other side of this wire. Just look at Luisa."

I looked up to Luisa; she smiled and waved me on.

Antonelli said, "You must make it to her. You must take a step. I am going to step backward now and pull the staff toward me. You will have to take a step when I do that, or you will fall. You must take a step. You must take a step now. Here I go."

Antonelli stepped backward. I let out a scream. The crowd gasped. I felt my foot on the wire. The crowd cheered.

"Don't listen to the crowd," Antonelli said. "Look to Luisa. Here we go. Another step. Small, bold steps. That's how you change. You must take another step. I'm stepping backward now."

He stepped backward again, and I felt my hands grasp the staff tighter. The crowd cheered again, louder this time. I felt my other foot on the wire. I had taken the step.

"One more time," Antonelli said.

"I can't," I murmured.

"You must. There is no turning back now. You're on the wire. You must take another step. I'm stepping backward now."

My foot touched down on the wire, and the crowd hooted and hollered.

Antonelli kept taking steps backward, and I kept following. I constantly put more pressure on the staff, relying on it for balance. Somehow, though, he managed to keep his balance and control me as well.

Before I knew it, Antonelli's back was just half a foot from Luisa.

"Now, listen," he said. "You've done it. You've gotten here all by yourself. Now I'm going to let go of the staff."

Panic shot through my body. I broke my look from Luisa. "No!" I looked at Antonelli and suddenly lost my balance. I leaned heavily on the left side of the staff and nearly fell off the wire. The crowd shrieked.

"Look at Luisa!" Antonelli's voice boomed.

I looked back at her and found my balance.

"Good," he continued. "Good. Now just keep looking at her. I'm going to bend down now, and then I'm going to let go of the staff. I want you to hand the staff to her. She needs it for balance now. When you hand it to her, raise your arms out to your sides like an airplane to keep your balance momentarily. Then I will stand and offer you my hands to use as balance. I'm going to bend down now."

I called out helplessly, "No!"

Antonelli knelt down. "Now I'm going to let go of the staff. When I do, you hand it to Luisa, nice and slowly. Don't break eye contact with her. Are you looking at her?"

"Yes," I murmured.

"Good, now hand her the staff."

Luisa reached out her arms. I handed it to her slowly and stood on my own. The crowd went wild.

Luisa turned and walked back toward the platform.

Antonelli stood up and smiled broadly. "Bravo! You did it. Now it's time to strike out on your own."

He took a step backward.

"No, wait!" I said, suddenly panicked.

"You can do it. Don't take your eyes off Luisa. No matter what. You don't need me now."

He slowly turned and walked away. The crowd groaned with worry for me.

Tears of helplessness welled in my eyes, and I blinked to push them back.

Antonelli reached the platform and stood with Luisa. They started clapping for me to move. The crowd followed suit.

I stared at Luisa. Her face changed suddenly into Meg's. "Prove it," she said.

I felt a surge of emotion and took a step forward. My foot didn't land squarely on the wire, and my body bowed to the right. The crowd screamed. I straightened. I took another step. The crowd's clapping and gasping sounded hollow, distant. Meg looked at me, unimpressed. "Drifter," she said.

Another step.

Luisa's face morphed back.

Another step.

Again I didn't place the middle of my foot on the wire.

I bowed to the right.

I swung my arms to catch my balance, but I overcorrected.

The crowd shrieked.

I felt my feet above my head.

A split-second before I hit the ground, a net rose to catch me.

18
THE LION TAMER

The net lowered me to the ground, and I felt an incredible sense of relief. The ringmaster ran over to me. The spotlight followed him. He hugged me, then raised my hand triumphantly.

"What do you think, folks? How about a hand for our volunteer!"

Everyone in the crowd stood up and cheered wildly. The ringmaster pointed upward to the Zanzinnis, who were now standing on a platform even higher than the one on which I had stood.

"And now, folks, the Zanzinnis will perform their world-famous, death-defying aerial acrobatics!"

The spotlight moved from the ringmaster and me up to the Zanzinnis. Luisa swung out from the platform on a trapeze bar.

The ringmaster nudged me. "Good work," he whispered.

"But I fell," I said.

"Of course you did. You'll do that when you start moving forward to your goals. But you made the attempt. You took bold steps. And you learned that when you fall, it isn't so bad. You started the heroic journey."

"I was scared to death, though. I just couldn't . . ."

Suddenly someone behind me grabbed my left arm, twisted it behind my back, and started shoving me forward, sending a sharp pain through my shoulder and neck.

"Larry!" the ringmaster cried out with surprise. "What are you doing?!"

"Just startin' a little early, mate," the person behind me said, revealing a deep Australian accent. I twisted to see a man wearing a safari shirt and a sweat-stained fedora. He forced me toward the left ring, shoving me forward while maintaining an unbreakable grip on my arm.

Stumbling and struggling to break free, I cried out, "Let me go!"

Within seconds, Larry had me in the left ring, standing at the gate of the cage I had seen earlier. He let my arm go and threw me violently to the ground inside the cage.

I spun around and screamed, "What the hell are you doing?!"

"You were acting like a pussy up there," Larry said sternly, pointing to the high wires. "So I thought you might as well be in here with your own kind." He motioned toward a small cage adjoining ours. Inside, six lions were feeding on bloody slabs of meat. The lions ripped into the meat as if they hadn't eaten in days, and their heads were covered in red. Between me and the lions were a lot of big, sturdy boxes and wooden balls, all part of an obstacle course that looked something like a jungle gym.

"No!" I screamed, realizing where I was. I jumped to my feet, pushed past Larry, and tried to exit the cage. The gate was locked. The wall of metal bars rose a good twenty-five feet high. There was no escape. I rattled the cage. "This isn't funny! Let me out!"

Henry must have seen the whole thing. He came hobbling up to the cage. "Larry!" he shouted. "No! Not this way! Let him out!"

I turned to find Larry standing in the middle of the cage, taking a whip off of his belt loop. "He can't change, Henry, because he keeps focusing on what he's scared of. He can't keep backing down or running from his fears. It's time for that man to stand up in life, or, for God's sake, at least find something bigger than himself to fight for."

"No, Larry! I'm telling you . . ." Henry responded, only to be cut off by the ringmaster's voice booming throughout the tent.

"Ladies and gentlemen, you are about to meet the bravest man on earth. A man who has tamed his fear and the *fiercest* animals on the planet. A man who handles more savage, untamed beasts in his shows than anyone else in the world would ever dare! It is with great pleasure that I introduce to you Larry the Lion Tamer!"

The spotlight hit Larry, and the crowd gave him a rousing welcome. He quickly circled the cage, cracking his whip several times in the direction of the lions. When he neared Henry and me, he grabbed my forearm and jerked me toward the center of the ring. "Sorry, Henry," he said.

Despite my resistance, Larry managed to yank me across the space and pushed me onto a large red box.

"Move and you die," he said. Then he circled the cage, cracked his whip several times again in the direction of the lions, and jumped onto the green box next to me.

The lion cage door lifted, and six lions bounded out and ran wildly around the cage. Several of them lunged toward us as they circled the ring, each time bringing gasps from the audience, and each time being driven back by the noise of Larry's whip snapping in the air.

"You see that one there?" Larry said, pointing to a massively maned beast circling the cage. "He's the one who did this." Larry quickly glanced down at his leg, then back to his charges. I followed his look and saw that his calf was terribly scarred. "We call him Mufasa, because he's the king," Larry said. "He really got a hold of me. Shook me like a rag doll during a show. The poor audience was terrified."

"The *audience* was terrified?!" I said. "You're crazy, Larry! I don't want any part of this. Let me out, *please.*"

Larry shook his head at me as if disappointed. Then he jumped off the box and cracked his whip toward the lions, sending them scurrying to the left.

"Life's like being in a lion cage, mate. Show fear, back down, or turn away from what's in front of you, and you're dead."

Larry advanced directly toward the lions, and the crowd moaned with concern. With a few shouts and some more cracks of the whip, though, he managed to get the lions to line up single file and sit on their haunches. He then made them walk across the top of the jungle gym and jump on and off the large wooden balls at a frenzied pace. He even made Mufasa walk up a seesaw centered over a triangular box, then down the other side as it tilted over.

As Mufasa stepped off the seesaw to my left, Larry walked over to me and pushed me off the box into the middle of the ring.

The crowd gasped.

"What are you doing!" I screamed in terror.

The ringmaster's voice filled the tent. "Ladies and gentlemen, our brave volunteer is ready to stand up to another monumental challenge!"

"No!" I screamed.

Larry hopped up onto the red box, threw his whip down in front of me, and said flatly, "Your turn."

"What!?" I took one look at Mufasa, then locked eyes with Larry. "No way! I don't want to do this, you hear me!?" I turned toward the gate of the cage and saw Henry searching through a ring of keys on the other side. "Henry!" I screamed as I ran toward him, hoping to get the hell out of there.

Just as I reached the gate, Henry looked over my shoulder with fright. "Watch your back!"

I spun around and saw the lions on the other side of the cage eyeing me curiously. Mufasa and two other lions began moving furtively in my direction. They looked up at Larry, then back at me, then took a step, then looked back at Larry, then back at me, then took another step.

"*I don't have the key!*" Henry cried out helplessly, his expression telling me I was done for.

Larry called to me, "You'd better start walking over here."

I looked at him in terror. "Larry, let me out! I told you, I don't want any part of this . . ."

"You're in it now," he said sternly. "You'd better start walking over toward me. *Now!*"

My legs trembled; I couldn't find my feet. The image of the lions tearing at the slabs of meat, their heads red with blood, filled my mind.

Mufasa and the other two continued to creep toward me.

"Get over here!" Larry said through his teeth.

The three advancing lions stopped at the sound of Larry's voice. They looked at him cautiously, but Mufasa didn't take his eyes off me and took another step. He was now even with Larry on the red box.

"Mufasa is going to attack you if you don't walk over here *like you belong here,*" Larry warned. "Now *walk!*"

I took a timid step forward; Mufasa stopped and cocked his head.

I took another step.

Mufasa lunged toward me.

"Mufasa, *no!*" Larry screamed.

Mufasa stopped about ten feet in front of me. I stared at him in terror. His mouth was open, and I could see the long, yellowed canines.

"He's going to charge you if you look at him that way!" Larry hollered.

"I don't know what to do!" I shrieked. The high, shrill sound of my voice was unrecognizable to me.

"If he charges, you stand tall and scream '*No!*' at him!"

"I can't do this!" I shouted.

Mufasa lunged again.

I dropped to the ground and covered my head.

I felt the lion's whole body run over me. Then a blunt blow to my leg sent me rolling.

Crack!

Larry's whip. *Thank God!*

I opened my eyes. Mufasa was standing six feet from me. He roared and flashed his fangs. His eyes were wild.

"Now, *damn you,* you better *stand up!*" Larry shouted at me.

I rose to my feet, whimpering, and backed up into the cage bars. Mufasa didn't take his eyes off me.

"He *will* attack you again if you don't *show your courage.* Take a step into him and scream at him to get back. Scream it with all your soul!" Larry called out.

Larry's voice seemed muffled to me. My heart beat so loudly that I could barely hear him or the crowd. I just looked at Mufasa in terror.

He lunged again. Spinning around, I gripped my head in fright. I felt a blunt swat on my shoulder and went sprawling to the ground in pain. I looked up, and Mufasa was already in the air, about to land on me. I put my hands over my head and felt his legs slam into mine. He swatted my arms and torso with his powerful paws.

Crack!

Mufasa sprang off me.

I looked through my forearms and saw him crouched and ready to attack, about ten feet in front of me.

"STAND UP OR DIE!" Larry screamed at the top of his lungs. "STAND UP!"

I got up to one knee. Suddenly, Mufasa looked to my right and roared. I turned my head. The ringmaster was thrusting Mary into the cage. She saw Mufasa and let out a high-pitched scream that nearly broke my eardrums.

Mufasa roared at her.

"Mary!" I screamed.

She didn't seem to notice me. She just froze and stared at the roaring beast.

"Mary!" I screamed again, and got to my feet.

Mufasa took a step toward her and roared again.

"HE'S GOING TO ATTACK HER!" Larry called out.

"NO!"

I ran between Mary and the lion.

Mufasa roared and lunged.

I raised my arms high in the air and screamed, "MUFASA, GET BACK!"

The lion landed right in front of me. His head actually butted into my legs. I barked again, "GET BACK, GET AWAY FROM HER, YOU BASTARD!"

Mufasa's eyes widened, and he stepped backward and roared at me and at Mary.

I stepped into him and pointed toward the other lions. "*Get back there!*"

Mufasa looked at me and cocked his head.

"*Get back now!*" I said, stepping into him once more.

The lion roared and showed his fangs.

I took another step toward him and screamed with all my might, "GET BACK NOW, YOU SON OF A—"

Suddenly, Mufasa backed up several feet. I charged two more steps toward him, and he turned and trotted back to the other lions.

"That's my boy!" Larry called out.

The crowd came to its feet, roaring louder than the lions.

I looked at Larry and the crowd wildly and felt the blood pumping furiously through my veins. I looked over my shoulder for Mary. . . .

She had disappeared.

I looked back at Larry.

"Something worth fighting for," he said.

19
THE STRONG MAN

The ringmaster opened the gate, and Larry and I emerged from the cage. The first person I saw was Henry. He hobbled toward Larry and embraced us both in a heartfelt hug.

"You did it!" he cheered.

Larry grabbed my hand and raised it in the air. The crowd was still going wild.

We headed for the aisle leading to the performers' area. Audience members threw popcorn on us like rice at a wedding. Throngs of people left their seats and patted us on the shoulder.

One of the security guards who had been standing at the entrance to the performers' area worked his way toward us and helped us get through the crowd. When we reached the flap, he and the other guard had to struggle to keep excited spectators at bay.

Inside the performers' area, everyone cheered ecstatically for us.

A man holding a handful of long wires tipped with what looked like small, charred marshmallows squeezed past us. He paused, looking at me. "Our hero! Hey, you wanna go back out there now and swallow some fire with me?"

Everyone paused and looked at me expectantly.

"No, thanks," I said. "After all the action, I'm already a bit burned out."

The room erupted in laughter.

After handshakes and backslaps from clowns, acrobats, jugglers, and hoop twirlers, Henry and I finally sat down on two stools in front of the mirrors. Both feeling a little exhausted, we simply sat watching the remaining performers preparing for their acts. There was an unspoken contentment and peace between us.

After a few minutes, Henry chuckled. "I thought Mufasa was going to eat you!"

I laughed. "You and I both!"

"You did good, sonny."

"Thank you, Henry."

"I'm proud of you. I knew you could do it. I knew that given the chance and the push, you would do it all—you would take bold steps forward on the tight rope. You would stand up against your fears in the lion cage. I just knew it."

I sighed. "I don't even think *I* knew it."

"But I bet now you have a newfound belief in what you're capable of, huh?"

"I do."

"Good. I really do think you're strong enough now to stand up to your own fears. There's just one more thing that might hold you back from changing."

"What's that?"

"Are you strong enough to stand up to other people who might prevent you from changing?"

"What do you mean?"

Henry called over a passing juggler. "Hey, Jerry, could you go track down big Mike for me? Tell him I want him to meet someone."

A few minutes later, a massive man walked over to us. He didn't really stand so much as *loom.* Over his huge, muscular bulk he wore a red-and-white-striped shirt, black tights, a big red belt, and black bands around his upper arms. Like everyone else in the park, he looked the part. His barrel chest resembled that of a bull, and his biceps were the size of bowling balls. He looked as if he could throw me across the room like a candy bar.

"Yo, Henry, Jerry said you needed me?" He looked down at me, and I just gaped in awe. He was truly the biggest human being I had ever seen.

Henry smiled. "Well, Mike, I was just wondering if you had a few minutes to talk to the kid here."

"Sure, Henry. About what?"

"I was hoping you might share your story with him. I think he's going to have to struggle to change when he gets back home—he might face the same things you did before you were Strong Man Mike."

Mike nodded and pulled up a stool, and as he sat I couldn't help worrying whether the legs of the stool would buckle and break. They didn't, but he presented an incongruous image—he looked like an ox sitting on a toothpick.

Mike sat for several moments, eyeing the ground as though lost in thought. He looked like someone about to undertake an extraordinarily complex task.

"I don't know your story," he said, "but maybe you can relate. I didn't always look like this"—he motioned with his baseball-mitt-size hands. "I wasn't always Strong Man Mike, jus' like Henry said. I was a small kid . . . real small.

"The story goes like this. I was born too early. Mom had me two full months before I was due. I was tiny, like a helpless little mouse. The doctors had to put me in a bubble for a few months to keep me alive. There were all sorts of complications. I had a weak heart, a collapsed lung, frail bone structure—stuff like that. I guess that for the first few years of my life my mom and dad were always worried I'd die. Even as I got older there were always trips to the hospital for one thing or another: growing pains, asthma, or just to get medication for everything else. The hospital trips were real hard because we lived way up in the mountains in a small logging town, and the hospital was in a bigger town down in the valley—it took about two hours to get there.

"Anyway, it's no good being a little mouse when your family runs a timber-cutting business. My dad and older brother, Tom, could have used another pair of hands when they were up in the woods, but Mom always made sure I stayed home so I wouldn't get hurt. I remember when I was around eight or nine years old, my folks got in a real scruff about me helping out. Dad wanted me to do simple things like haul saws and chains from the trucks to the trees, but Mom was too worried about my weak heart and asthma to let me do anything like that.

"Because I couldn't help, life was not easy for my brother Tom. He had to do a lot of work. He was only four years older than me, but he always looked like an adult because of all the manual labor he did.

"That came in handy, though, when I hit high school. I was always being picked on because I was so small. Tom, who was a senior by then, would always save the day when I was about to get creamed after school. He was a real guardian angel, the miracle that allowed me to get through freshman year alive."

Mike paused and fidgeted on the stool as if he didn't know what to do with his arms. Finally he folded them across his chest and continued, without ever taking his eyes off the floor.

"That summer Dad finally convinced Mom that I should be able to help out. He said that at fifteen years old a boy becomes a man. I was excited to be more helpful—and to be out from under Mom's wing too. Of course, Dad and Tom still protected me quite a bit. Instead of felling trees with a chainsaw, though, or setting chokers on logs, I got to drive the log truck, or clean equipment, or cut branches or knots off the fallen logs. That summer was the best of my life. I loved being up the mountain with Dad and Tom. It made me feel like a man.

"On one of the last days of the season, there was a big thunderstorm. Dad, Tom, and I scrambled to get all the equipment into the bed of the pickup and the logs onto the truck. By the time we did, the rain was coming down in sheets. Dad told Tom to drive the pickup back home as fast and safely as he could to let Mom know we were okay and coming home. Dad and I always rode together in the log truck—guess he always wanted me around him so he could keep me safe.

"To this day I have never seen a thunderstorm so bad. The rain was coming down so hard that Dad wouldn't even let me drive—and he was always trying to get me to drive so I could feel like I was being helpful. The dirt road leading down the mountain was steep and treacherous.

There were deep, water-filled potholes everywhere. In a lot of spots, little rivers of rainwater were running over the road, and the ditches along each side were beginning to fill with water.

"We were practically crawling down the mountain. About halfway down, we started to hear an odd squeaking noise from the back of the truck. Dad pulled over. Even as slow as we were moving, with all the weight of the logs on the truck, we came to a sliding stop—the road was that muddy.

"Dad said, 'Stay inside the cab, son. I don't want you catching cold. I'm gonna check the winches.' He jumped out of the truck, and a few moments later I heard a snap and a scream. I felt a powerful rocking and looked in the side mirror—logs were falling off the truck."

Mike paused and wrung his hands.

"I threw my door open and jumped out of the cab, screaming for my dad. He didn't answer. A couple more logs rolled off the truck and into the ditch at the side of the road. I followed them with my eyes, and that's when I saw Dad. He was pinned under a bunch of logs in the ditch. His face was covered in blood and mud. I screamed and ran into the ditch. The rainwater runoff was already up to my shins. Kneeling down, I tried to get to Dad through the four or five logs that were on top of him, but I couldn't reach him. I screamed, 'Dad, Dad! Are you okay?'

"He opened his eyes and looked at me. He was scared. I had never seen him scared before. Water was running over his legs and waist. He tried to move his arms and screamed in pain. He looked up at me helplessly and said, 'Son, I can't move.'

"I said, 'Dad, I'll get you out.' I stood up and wrapped my arms around the log on top of him. I put my whole body, my whole soul, into lifting it. It didn't budge. I changed my position and tried again. Still I couldn't budge it. I looked down at Dad. The water was now up to his chest. I ran around the other side of the log and tried to lift it again. I pulled and I pushed and I cried and I screamed for God's help to move that log. I tore the skin on my hands and forearms trying to get a grip on it, trying to twist it or roll it or lift it, but I couldn't budge it.

"Then Dad screamed for me. I ran back to the other side, where I could see his face. Water was up to his neck. He looked at me . . ."

Mike stopped ringing his hands and lifted them to his face. He sat silent for a few moments. Henry reached over and touched his shoulder, and Mike looked up at him and nodded. The giant was crying.

He looked back to the ground and cleared his throat. "My dad looked at me with the eyes of a man who knew his time had come. He seemed almost peaceful about it. He smiled at me and blinked the tears from his eyes. He said, 'Son, it's okay. Don't you worry. It's not your fault. No man could have gotten these logs off of me. It's not your fault. You tell your ma that I loved her all my life, okay? You do that for me, okay?' I told him I would. Then he said, 'You tell Tom I'm proud of him, okay?' I said I would. Then he said, 'Son . . . Mikey . . . I'm proud of you too. Don't let anyone ever tell you you're not strong enough or you're not good enough. You can do the same things the other kids do. You hear me?' I cried and said I did. Then he said, 'I love you, son. I'm so proud of my boy. I'm so proud of you.'

"Then," Mike said quietly, "I watched my father drown."

Saying he needed some air, Mike walked through the tent flap to the animal cage area outside. Henry and I sat silently for a few minutes, then walked out to meet him. He was sitting on the back of a wagon full of hay. As we approached him, a lump still remained in my throat.

Mike looked up at me for the first time. "Now, let me finish my story, so I can tell you the lesson Henry wants you to get. After my dad's funeral, I made a decision in my life. I decided I would never be weak again. I decided to change everything in my life. No more excuses about not lifting or carrying things. No more excuses about not working out or running and playing. I set a goal to be as physically strong as I possibly could—not out of remorse or self-hatred for what happened to my father, but because of his inspiring last words. I could be as strong as anyone else and as strong as I wanted to be. I committed to being that. I had it set in my mind that I could be so much more than a mouse.

"But the rest of the world wasn't so keen on the idea. When I started lifting heavier equipment at work, Tom said, 'Mikey, you don't have to push yourself. Be careful.' When

I started lifting weights in high school, Mom begged me to stop and was always telling me I was going to hurt myself. When I tried to join the wrestling team, the coach said, 'Don't get your hopes up, kid.' Even after I made the team, he and other people would say, 'You're too weak to ever be good.' The few friends I had—those like me, who always got beat up after school—started asking, 'Who do you think you are?' and 'What are you trying to prove?' It was like everyone had labeled me long ago as 'the weak kid,' and they just couldn't accept that I might want to be more than that, or that I *could* be more than that.

"Now, of course, many people were just trying to look out for me. Mom and Tom just didn't want to see me get hurt. I'm sure some of my teachers and friends and coaches felt the same way. But what they didn't know was that they were sending me messages that encouraged me to be weak. And of course, there were some people, like my old friends, who were just a little jealous that I was getting stronger than them. Over the next ten years, as I got stronger and stronger, I either won people's support for trying to be the strongest and healthiest I could, or I had to cut some ties. I lost a few friends along the way because they couldn't understand what I was trying to do. I even left my hometown so I could be around more people who wanted to live their life at the level I was trying to live mine at. But most people who cared about me came around to the idea that I was doing what was right for me. I just had to be patient with them and let them know that I loved them and that I wouldn't outgrow them.

"So here's my lesson: We all get to a point where we decide to become stronger. When we start that process, a lot of people unknowingly stop our progress by trying to protect us or to keep us living according to the label they've created for us. If I had listened to my mom or my brother or my friends or my coaches, I would be a small, frail, weak kid who secretly despised himself for being that. Instead, I listened to those who encouraged me—like my dad—and I listened to my inner desires. I became who I wanted to be because I didn't get trapped in other people's ideas of who I *should* be. *That* is how I went from mouse to Strong Man Mike."

Henry and I sat in the front row for Mike's performance. He juggled sixteen-pound bowling balls, lifted the front end of a car full of clowns off the ground, let an elephant step on his chest, and performed other feats of strength that blew the audience's mind.

During his last act, a forklift brought in an eight-foot tree trunk two feet thick and set it in front of him. Mike asked another audience member and me to try to lift it. We stood at either end and lifted with everything we had. It didn't move.

Then Mike reached down, scooped up the log, and hoisted it onto his shoulders with barely a grunt.

The crowd oohed and aahed.

For the first time since I had met him, Mike smiled.

20
THE CENTER RING

After Strong Man Mike finished his show, the ringmaster asked all the evening's performers to come to the center ring. As a stream of jugglers, clowns, trapeze artists, dancers, trainers, and others flowed from the performers' area to the center ring, the ringmaster said, "Ladies and gentlemen, I would like to thank you for coming to our show this evening. I hope each and every one of you saw something tonight that reminded you of the wonder and possibility in this world. Now please join me in giving a hand to all of tonight's performers, who, by showing us their talent and potential, always remind us of our own."

The audience rose to its feet and whistled and clapped joyously. Larry the Lion Tamer pulled Henry and me out of our seats and made us stand in the center ring as well. I felt awkward and out of place, so I looked to the other performers for what to do. They waved and blew kisses at the crowd. What the hell, I thought, and blew kisses too. The performers turned in circles to wave and bow to every section of the bleachers encircling the center ring, and I followed suit.

Henry whispered in my ear, "Look at them all. Look at the expressions on the people's faces."

Everyone in the audience was smiling and clapping excitedly.

After a few moments the ringmaster said, "Thank you, everyone. Our performers will stay down here if you would like to meet them personally. Thank you all again for coming, and we hope to see you again soon. God bless, and good night!"

After the last audience members waved their final farewell from the exit to all of us in the center ring and then disappeared through the tent flap, the performers broke out in celebration. They cheered and hugged and slapped one another on the back, then turned inward in the center ring and all embraced in a huge group hug. Then they all simultaneously turned around and faced the empty seats. Their cheers and glad chatter fell silent as they gazed into the bleachers with expressions of contentment—or maybe it was appreciation. A minute passed . . . then another.

And another.

I turned to Henry and whispered, "What's going on?"

He didn't respond. He too just stared into the empty seats.

Another minute passed, and then, in another simultaneous movement, all the performers stepped out of the center ring and suddenly vanished into thin air.

I spun and looked around me. Only Henry and I stood in the center ring.

"Where'd they go?" I asked.

Henry smiled at me. "Their work is done."

"What work?"

Henry didn't answer. He just paced around the center ring, staring off into the empty seats. When he had walked the entire perimeter, he headed to the middle of the center ring.

"You asked, what work?" Henry said quietly. "What work do you think everyone was doing in this ring tonight?"

"Well, they're all performers—they were entertaining."

"Entertaining?" Henry asked doubtfully. "So would you describe what Larry the Lion Tamer and Strong Man Mike and the Zanzinni family did for you tonight as just entertaining?"

"Well, no ... no, I wouldn't. ... They did much more than that."

"What did they do?"

"I guess they ... I don't know how to describe it. The Zanzinnis pushed me to be bold. Larry scared me and made me stand up to my fears. Mike inspired me to remain strong."

"And does that sound like the work of entertaining to you?"

"No, it doesn't."

"Well, what kind of work *does* it sound like?"

I thought for a long moment. "I would have to say, the work of ... just making a difference."

"Ahh," Henry said approvingly. "I like that, the work of making a difference. Indeed, that is what these people do. Each of them stands in the center ring, not to be under the spotlight or to feel the adoration of the audience, but to make a difference. Their work is not about themselves; each one knows full well that he or she is but one soul in the middle of a thousand others. No, these people do their work for no other reason than to make others smile. They do their work so that others can have a break from their day and feel, even if for but a moment, a sense of magic and hope. They do it to remind others of the possibilities in this world: that maybe they too can juggle all of life's hassles successfully; that maybe they too can tame their fears; that maybe they too have more strength within them than anyone could ever have imagined. Every performer here tonight gave all they could give, for no other reason than to make a difference. That, to me, makes them miracle workers."

"But where did they all go?" I asked.

"Oh," Henry said, smiling at me, "who's to say? You can't wonder where miracles go or where they come from—you just have to be thankful for them when they arrive, and thankful for them after they have departed."

Henry coughed violently again. This time he bent over in pain. When his fit stopped, he looked up at me apologetically. He glanced around the Big Tent and nodded, as if hearing someone's voice. "And now, my friend, I believe it is time for me to leave too. It's time for my last lesson to you."

I looked at Henry in confusion and shook my head. "What? Leave? You can't leave. I . . . I still need you. I haven't gotten any answers yet."

Henry smiled at me. "Oh, I'm sure you've gotten plenty of answers on this journey."

I shook my head again. "Yes, I have. But no. I mean, yes, I've found many answers . . . but not all the ones I've been looking for. I don't know what happened to Mary. I don't know the significance of the envelope. I don't know why you've been helping me. I don't know why all this has—"

Henry raised his hand. "Hush," he said. "Patience. Like I said, I have one last lesson for you. Maybe that lesson will give you a few answers."

He smiled and paced around me. "Let me return to what I was saying about the performers. I believe they have something to teach us. You see, many of us live our lives desperately seeking to draw attention to ourselves. We live our lives to be noticed, accepted, and adored. We live our lives as if we were in the center ring, as if the world should sit around applauding our every move. But there are a small number of people in this world who live their lives to make others smile, to remind others of the magic and hope in the world, to help them discover the possibilities that live within them. Whenever people like this end up in the spotlight, they use their moment to help others through the dark. These people are the miracle workers. These are the people who embody the last lesson I will now give you."

Henry looked upward, and all the lights in the Big Tent went out. Then a soft spotlight beam lit the area where we stood in the middle of the center ring. A second later, two similar lights lit the smaller rings intersecting the center ring on the left and right.

"Pretend with me for a moment that the ring we now stand in is the present. The small ring to our left is the past; the small ring to our right is the future. I believe that the brightness of your life experience at any one time will always be based upon how you look at these three rings. Let me tell you how most people live their lives. They look to the ring on the left and say, 'Look what happened to me in the past. Why did it all happen? What did I get out of it?' They look to the center ring and say, 'What's happening to me right now? Why is it all happening, and what am I getting out of it?' They look to the ring on the right and say, 'What will happen to me in the future? How will I end up? What will I get?'"

As Henry spoke, the spotlight beam above us dimmed. He smiled to me and pointed toward the left ring. I glanced back over to it and froze.

Inside the ring stood nearly everyone who had ever been important in my life. My dad, mom, grandpa, and grandma were there. My close friends from high school and college were there. My former co-workers, girlfriends, teachers, and mentors were there. They all stared at me without expression.

Henry motioned toward them all. "You see those people? Most of your life you have looked at them and the events you endured with them, and asked yourself, 'Why did I have to go through all that? What's the meaning of it all? What did I get out of my experiences with all those people?'"

He walked in front of me. "Would you agree that at some level you asked questions like those?"

I looked to the ring of people and saw that they were looking back at me expectantly.

"Yes."

Henry nodded. "Now, let me ask you this. Did you ever ask yourself, 'What did I make happen for those people? What did I *give?*'"

I knew the answer, but didn't want to say it.

Henry grabbed my arm and walked me to the edge of the ring. "Look at their faces," he commanded sternly. "Did you ever ask, 'What did I *give?*'"

I looked to the ring again. My family continued to look at me expectantly. My friends cocked an eyebrow and waited. My former girlfriends crossed their arms.

I half laughed, half coughed. "I did my best to . . ."

Taking me by the shoulders, Henry peered at me intently. "Did you ever ask the question?"

I shook my head. "No."

The lights above the left ring went out. The people disappeared.

I looked to Henry. "What is this, a guilt trip?"

Henry looked at me flatly. "I didn't ask you to feel guilty. I asked if you ever asked yourself what you gave."

Henry circled me, and the lights in the Big Tent went out once more.

When they came back on, I stood in a crowd of people all facing toward the middle of the center ring. I pushed through the crowd to see what they were looking at. I didn't recognize any of the people—until I got to the middle. There I saw myself sitting at a desk. Henry stood to one side, watching me at the desk.

"And that guy—do you think he's asking himself, 'What's happening to me right now? Why is it all happening, and what am I getting out of it?'"

I nodded.

Henry pointed to the people surrounding the desk. Suddenly I saw co-workers and friends. Mary and her family stood on the other side of me.

Henry then pointed to me at the desk once more. "And do you think that guy is asking himself, 'What am I making happen in my life? What am I *giving* right now?'"

I shook my head.

The Big Tent went dark.

"You see where I'm going with this?" Henry said, standing somewhere in front of me.

"Yeah, but . . . who were all those people?" I asked.

A dim spotlight illumined the center ring once more. Henry and I stood alone.

"Those were people you interact with practically every day or so. Some were the people who work at your local grocery store, library, coffee stop, and gas station. Others were people you pass on the street on a regular basis. Others were people in your community who have asked for your help. All were people that you barely ever notice or thank or make smile. They were people who somehow give to you but who have never received a thing back from you, not even a thank-you."

"Henry, that's not exactly fair," I said. "I can't make a difference in the life of *every single* person I meet or happen to walk by!"

Henry shook his head. "You're right. I'm sorry. Would you mind, then, telling me just *one single person* you do that for?"

I opened my mouth to defend myself, then stopped. He was right.

The light above us dimmed lower.

Henry pointed to the ring on the right. "You know where this is going?"

I nodded. "The future. I've always worried what would happen to me, what I'd end up with or get tomorrow, not what I would make happen or give to others." I let out a deep breath and shook my head. "That's what you're saying. That's the truth, isn't it?"

Henry looked at me sadly, and then the lights went out.

~~~

After a few moments of darkness and silence, Henry spoke. "You see, most people, maybe including you, have lived life as if they were at the whim of circumstance and as if they were supposed to get something from the world. The miracle makers in this world, though, are the people who *live by choice* and *live to contribute.* They ask what they're making happen, and they ask what they're giving. I think that you've probably learned a lot about living by choice in your time here at the park. My final lesson to you, then, is about contribution, and it says simply this: if you want your life experience to be bright, choose to contribute."

Suddenly, the spotlight above the center ring came on once again, this time with full intensity.

Henry was standing at the intersection of the center ring and the ring to its left. He waved at me to join him.

As I neared him he said, "I don't speak of that lesson halfheartedly; I hope you've sensed that. I've tried to contribute to your life. I've tried to make a difference. I hope that I have."

"You have, Henry. Of course you have."

He smiled. "Good. I'm happy I could help. I think you are—"

"But *why* did you help, Henry? From what everyone has told me, it was some kind of big deal."

Henry shifted his stance. "Well, you know, helping is always a big deal. Sometimes you have to sacrifice your time and energy. You've got to . . ."

"No, Henry, no more lessons. Why did *you* help *me?* What did you sacrifice?"

Henry reached out and squeezed my arm. "Well, look who is suddenly strong and in command of the conversation! That lion taming got into your heart, didn't it?"

I nodded, then raised my eyebrows expectantly.

"Okay, okay," Henry said, recognizing that I wasn't going to let it go. "I helped you because I knew I could. Simple as that. I've been here at this park a long time. When I saw that envelope, I knew something had gone wrong, and I knew I could figure it out. I knew I *had* to figure it out—for your sake and for the sake of the thousands of others who will come here after you."

"And what did that decision cost you? If so many people come here, why is it such a big deal for you to help me?"

Henry paused and held back a cough. "Because ... because even miracles have their beginnings and ends. Like I said, I've been here a long time. No miracle is intended to last forever, and I knew my time was up— so did everyone else. I knew I had one more miracle in me, and then ..."

Henry looked out toward the bleachers and kicked the soft dirt beneath his shoes.

"Then what?" I asked.

"Then ... well, I don't know. None of us know what happens to us when our time is done. All we know here at the park is that when someone's time is done, they walk out of this ring and disappear forever. The performers you saw tonight will come back again tomorrow because they have more miracles within them. Me? Well, when I walk out of this ring tonight, that's it."

Henry looked at me thoughtfully. "I chose you to be my last miracle."

21
THE LAST RIDE

Henry and I stood in silence for several moments. Then the spotlight above us dimmed.

Henry looked up and sighed. "It's time for me to complete my miracle."

"Wait!" I cried out, surprising myself with the urgency in my voice. A thousand questions flashed in my mind. What would happen to Henry? Where would he go? Where had the other performers gone? What was this place? But this all paled in comparison to the most important question of all.

"*What happened to Mary?* Before this is all over, Henry—whatever this *is*—I have to know what happened. You said thousands of people have come here or will come here to experience something similar to what I experienced. Is that what happened to Mary? Did she go through the same things as I did?"

Henry nodded. "Similar lessons, yes. But all relevant to her life."

"So what happened to her then? You said you could figure out what went wrong." I looked at Henry anxiously. "Did you?"

He nodded. "I did. Something went terribly wrong on one of the rides. But I can't tell you what went wrong. You'll have to see for yourself." He paused and peered into the left ring. "Now it's time for me to finish my work. . . ."

"But I have so many—"

"Tell me," Henry interrupted loudly, "who would you say is the person who cared about you most in life?"

I heard his question but wanted to stop whatever was happening. I had too many questions. "Henry, I—"

"Who cared about you the most?" Henry asked again. He put a hand on my shoulder and looked into my eyes intently.

"My mom."

Henry smiled. "That's what I thought."

He turned and looked into the left ring once more. I followed his gaze.

My mom stood in the middle of the ring. She looked exactly as she had on the day of my barbecue, the day of the car accident. She walked toward us and stopped at the intersection of the two rings.

"Hi, honey," she said to me.

I looked at her with almost no emotion. I figured she was a mirage or something like Mary had been, or that in the blink of a spotlight she would disappear.

Then she stepped into the center ring and hugged me. I felt her arms around me. I felt her heart beating. I smelled her perfume. She was real.

"Mom?" I asked, pulling her in close. I squeezed her as hard as I could to see if she was real. Earlier, at the Truth Booth, all I wanted to do was hug her. All my life, all I've wanted to do was hug her once more. "Mom? Is it really you?"

"Yes, honey," she said, embracing me tightly, "and I have something to give you. But first, do you remember the promise you made to me earlier?"

I tried to say yes, but the lump in my throat stopped the sound. I nodded my head.

"Good. I'm glad," she said happily. "Now, I have something to remind you of that promise. I want you to keep it with you as long as you keep that promise, okay?"

Mom pulled away from me and handed me an envelope. She smiled and stepped back into the left ring. "I'm proud of you, son. I'm proud of how far you've come. Now, keep hold of that envelope and don't open it until you're told, okay?"

I nodded and wiped the tears from my eyes. I looked at her standing in the left ring and felt terribly empty. I stepped toward her.

She raised her hand, stopping me. "It's okay, son. You just stay there. Right there in the present. That's where you belong now. That's where you'll fulfill your promise." She looked at me and smiled with tears in her eyes. "Live your life, honey. I love you."

The spotlight above her faded, and she disappeared.

Tears filled my eyes, and I had to bite my lip not to lose all control. I looked down at the envelope, then pulled Mary's envelope out of my back pocket. They were the same size and color, except that Mary's was stained with blood.

I looked up for Henry and saw him hobbling slowly across the center ring, toward the exit aisle.

"Wait! Henry!" I ran and caught up to him. I held out the envelope Mom had just given me. "It's the same envelope Mary received, isn't it?"

"It is," he said. His voice was frail and wispy, and his face was so pale, it looked as if he were about to pass out.

"Henry, are you okay?"

He smiled and kept trudging toward the exit.

"Henry. The envelope. Mary got it in the same way I did? By someone she thought cared about her the most?"

Henry nodded. "Her little brother."

I stopped walking. I could imagine Mary breaking down when she saw her little brother again, when he gave her the envelope.

"What's in the envelope, Henry? Why didn't Mary ever open it? Why did she give it to me? Why did she ask me to give it to her brother?"

Henry eyed the ground carefully as he continued slowly toward the edge of the center ring. "I'm afraid it is not yet time for you to know what the envelope contains. Why didn't Mary open her envelope? Because she was never told to. Just like your mother told you not to open the envelope until you were instructed to, Todd told her not to open hers. Because she never finished her journey here, no one had the chance to tell her to open the envelope. Why did she give her envelope to you? Because she thought she knew what it contained."

Henry stopped and looked at me. "Do you remember why I had to vouch for you to get in the park?"

"Yes. I didn't have an invitation."

"Exactly. You see, everyone who comes here has been invited, just as you heard the wizard say when you began this journey. Everyone who comes has received a ticket from someone who cares about them; that ticket gets them inside this magical place. Mary received a ticket from someone too. My guess is that she thought the envelope contained the invitation, and that's why she gave it to you. Just as she told you, she wanted you to experience this place."

I thought for a moment, trying to digest what he had said. A question came to my mind. "Who gave her the invitation?"

Henry shook his head and said, "I don't know," then started shuffling again to the edge of the center ring.

"But why would she want me to give the envelope to her brother?"

"I don't know. Maybe she was delusional after the accident. Since her brother had given her the envelope, maybe she was thinking of him. I don't know."

Henry reached the edge of the center ring and peered at the dirt on the other side. He looked at me with a serene gaze. "It's time for me to go."

"Wait!" I said, my mind still reeling with questions. "Henry, please, don't go. I still don't know what happened to Mary. Why didn't she finish this?"

Henry looked at the border of the center ring and didn't answer. He looked as if he were about to fall asleep.

"Henry?" I asked, shaking his shoulder.

He looked up at me as if waking from a dream. Then he said plainly, "Everyone gets one last ride before they leave to go home; then they open their envelope on the way out. That's the best part of an amusement park: the last ride. Mary never finished her ride, so she never opened her envelope."

"What ride, Henry? Why didn't she finish her last ride?"

Henry looked up to the exit of the tent.

"Crank is outside waiting for you. He'll take you to her last ride."

Henry turned to me and weakly stuck out his hand for me to shake it. "It's time for me to go."

"No!" I cried. "I'm not ready." I thought about all I'd been through, all the questions I still had. I wasn't sure if I could face what happened to Mary without Henry by my side. "You can't go, Henry. You can't go."

Henry stepped into me and gave me a gentle hug, then whispered in my ear, "Thank you, kiddo. You did good here. If it weren't for you, we would have never discovered a mistake in the miracle."

He pulled back, tears in his eyes. "You remember your promise to your mom—you always keep in mind the fact that you can be whoever you want to be and you can do whatever you want to do. And don't you open that envelope until you're told."

He stepped to the center ring's edge, and I reached out and grabbed his elbow. I looked at him urgently and then realized I didn't know what else to say. I felt tears stinging my eyes. My voice wavered. "Henry, I . . . I don't know how to thank you. . . . I can't even begin to . . ." I stopped and stared at him apologetically.

Henry reached up and gently released my hand from his elbow. "I know, kid. Don't worry about it. You're welcome." He patted my hand, then let it go. "Listen, I'm proud of you. I'm happy you were my last."

He smiled lovingly, stepped over the edge of the ring, and vanished.

Crank stood outside the tent, fidgeting with his tool belt. When he noticed me standing at the exit, I tried to say hello. All that came out, though, was, "Henry's gone."

Crank nodded. "I know. It's okay. I got to say my good-byes to him earlier. We all did."

We walked in silence around the corner where the animal cages were, then up the walkway between the bumper boats and the Hall of Mirrors. I was so lost in thought that I didn't realize all the crowds were gone until we passed the merry-go-round. It wasn't running. Neither was the Cyclone. The park was eerily silent again. The dirt and rocks beneath our shoes seemed to echo for miles into the night air as we continued walking north toward the mountain.

The walkway veered right at a group of tall pine trees just past the pirate ship, where it intersected with the end of the midway and opened into the grassy field where Harsh the Hypnotist's tent stood.

Crank led me onto a small dirt path that encircled the field. We followed the path past the field and into a wooded area at the base of the mountain. The lights mounted on the poles surrounding the field didn't quite reach the spot where we stood, so Crank pulled a flashlight from his tool belt and illuminated the path ahead. I could see that the path dropped a few feet and then opened to a small dock on a pond.

"There," he said, aiming the flashlight at an archway and sign above the dock, "is where things went wrong for Mary."

The sign above the dock read TUNNEL OF LOVE.

We climbed into the two-seat paddleboat moored to the dock. "Listen up, cutie pie," Crank said. "Don't think for a second you're going to get any action from me." He laughed and flashed his light into the crystal-clear water in front of us, illuminating tracks just below the surface. "You won't have to do any paddling— this here's automated now. We used to let couples just paddle into the tunnel, but they'd stay in there all night making out and causing traffic jams. So we ended up shutting down the ride and setting it up on tracks so that we could control the pace. To do it we had to drain as much of the water out of the pond as we could, then lay in the tracking. It was a nightmare. I was soaking wet for a year helping build this thing. That's why Henry asked me to take you—I know every inch of this ride."

"So this is the ride Mary chose as her last?"

"Yep," Crank said. "In the end, love is always the last ride."

"Do you know what happened to Mary here?"

"I've got an idea, but I can't be sure. I've checked out the ride a dozen times since Henry told me to, but I haven't found a single problem. But, see, this ride, like all the others, is different for everyone who goes on it. I'm hoping that by riding it with you, we can find out what happened to Mary. Since Henry says you two were lovers, you should have a similar experience in there. You *were* in love, right?"

I nodded.

"Good." Crank reached for a small box on the dock, which was connected to a thick electric cable. He pressed a green button, and our boat lurched forward.

"Here we go!" he said.

Our boat floated gently forward into the pond and toward the dark mouth of a tunnel in the base of the mountain.

I looked at the tunnel and asked, "Is there lighting in there? Will we be able to see?"

"You'll see what your heart has seen and needs to see," he replied softly.

Crank left his flashlight on for the first ten yards or so into the tunnel. The stone walls were low, narrow, and wet. I felt claustrophobic.

Crank turned off his flashlight. "Keep your eyes open."

The tunnel was an eerie black. My senses sharpened, and I felt the damp, cool air cause the hair on my arms to stand up. I heard water running and trickling all around us. There was a musty mildew smell. I felt my own heart beating softly.

"Look!" Crank said.

I couldn't see anything.

"Look!" he said again.

Up ahead of us I saw a little glow of light appear and disappear, like a firefly. I squinted my eyes.

Another glow, this time closer.

Another, closer . . .

Then the tunnel walls started glowing a deep purple, just bright enough that I could see the tip of my nose. Our boat was picking up speed. The walls started changing colors: bluish black ... purple again ... fuchsia ... pink. The colors started swirling all together.

Our boat picked up more speed. The waves of water being pushed aside by the boat made an almost deafening roar, and the glowing colors of the walls began to swirl into images:

My mom held me in her arms as an infant. Her voice suddenly boomed throughout the tunnel. "You're such a beautiful baby. ... I love you, son."

My dad held my hand at a park when I was small, and laughed when I picked up a turtle and put it back down. His voice echoed with my mother's. "Hey, my little turtle, did I ever tell you I love you?"

My grandpa hugged me and then lifted me over his head. "You're such a good boy! I love you!"

My grandma sat me atop a horse and smiled. "I'm so happy you're here. I love you!"

The boat lurched forward again.

The color of the tunnel walls blurred together faster.

I saw myself standing next to the car I owned in high school. My first girlfriend leaned in and kissed me. Her whisper exploded throughout the tunnel. "I love you."

I leaned across a table and took the hands of my college sweetheart. "I love you too," her voice blasted.

I embraced my best friend on graduation day. "We'll keep in touch—love you, man," he said.

The boat surged ahead; the walls of the tunnel churned a deep purple, then pink, then blue.

Mary's face flashed on the walls; the colors churned faster.

She and I are in bed. "I love you," she says, and snuggles against my chest.

We're at her parents' dinner table. She leans over. "Thank you for being such a good man. I love you."

We're standing side by side at the sink, brushing our teeth. "I wuvvv uuuu," she mumbles.

We're embracing after I proposed. "I love you," she says, her face full of tears.

The boat plunged on ahead again, faster.

Water started flying off the bow, into my lap and onto my face. The walls turned a dark red.

Images of Mary and me fighting started flashing on the walls . . . thousands of images. The sounds of hundreds of arguments blasted through the tunnel and deafened my ears.

"What's going on?!" I screamed to Crank.

He didn't reply.

I heard the sound of roaring water mix with the sounds of the arguments.

The images on the walls all bled together, and a new image appeared.

Mary is sitting at a table with a crystal ball on top of it. She is crying profusely.

"Should I leave him?" she asks.

Meg's face blurs into focus on the walls. "Yes," she says. "He'll never change. He's a drifter."

Mary bursts into tears.

"*No!*" I heard myself scream over the noise of the water and the echoes bouncing around the tunnel.

"Oh, no," I heard Crank say. "It was *Meg.* She caused this. *She killed love!*"

"What?!" I yelled, my heart and mind racing.

"Meg told Mary to leave you! She derailed love. That's where it all went wrong."

A wave of water crashed into our boat from the left, and I heard a loud pop.

"The tracks!" Crank screamed.

The rushing water lifted our boat and sent it sideways down another tunnel. Water flowed over our laps. The boat was sinking. The walls stopped glowing. It was pitch-black.

"What's happening?!" I screamed.

Our boat turned over with the flow of water, dumping us into the current. I was slammed into the walls of the tunnel by the force of the water. I fought to keep my head above the rushing water.

"Crank!"

No reply.

I heard the roar of the water getting louder ahead of us, then saw a light coming from around the corner. It looked like moonlight.

"It's the end!" Crank screamed from somewhere far behind me.

The current took me around a corner, and I could see a small opening into the night ahead of me.

The walls narrowed, and the current shot me out of the opening like water from a fire hydrant. I hit the ground, and the stream of water behind me sent me rolling down a hill of leaves and twigs and mud. I ended up in a small ravine next to a road, gasping for air and looking back in the direction I had come from. A forceful stream of water was shooting out a narrow cave entrance in the side of the mountain.

I heard Crank screaming from inside the cave, and suddenly he shot out of its mouth. The water pushed him down the hill with great force and washed him just past me and up onto the road.

I heard the sound of a truck.

"*No!*"

Crank stood over me lying in the ditch. His face was full of mud, but he smiled.

A horn blared.

"Now you know what happened to Mary," Crank said.

The horn blared again, making me wince. When I opened my eyes, a semi plowed through Crank.

"*Nooo!*" I screamed.

The truck's brakes squealed and smoked. I pulled myself to my feet and hobbled quickly toward it.

The driver jumped out, wide-eyed.

"You hit him!" I screamed.

He stared at me in shock.

Rounding the front of the truck, I expected to see Crank lying mangled on the road. He wasn't there.

"Hit who, mister?" The driver looked at me as if I were a madman. "I didn't hit anyone," he said. "I just saw you lying by the road and stopped to see if you were okay. Are you all right?

22
OPENING THE ENVELOPE

The truck driver turned the ignition key, and the engine roared to life.

"Are you sure about this?" he asked.

"Yes, I am. Thanks."

He nodded and handed me the flashlight I had asked for. I flipped it on and backed away from the driver's-side door. He closed it, looked at me through the window, and gave me a salute good-bye. The engine growled, and the truck pulled away.

A small stream of water was still pouring from the mouth of the cave in the mountainside, though it was nothing like the fire-hydrant force that had pushed Crank and me out into the night. I aimed the flashlight into the opening and started second-guessing myself. *No, you've got to go back.*

I climbed inside the cave. The water was up to my knees, but the current was much weaker now. I slogged against it for about a hundred yards, then felt my foot hit something under water. I pointed the flashlight downward.

Tracks.

I swept the walls around me with the flashlight beam. This was where our boat had been knocked off the tracks by the surge of water.

I turned left and followed the tracks back the way we had come. The darkness of the tunnel made me feel claustrophobic again. I shined my flashlight onto the walls and reached up and touched them. They were just stone.

After walking and wading through the tunnel for what seemed an eternity, I saw moonlight shining ahead. I flicked off the flashlight and hurried onward.

I climbed up, exhausted, onto the dock and sat for a few minutes, catching my breath; then I wrung the water out of my pant legs and shook the water out of my shoes. Glancing back toward the tunnel opening, I noticed that the pond water was layered with algae floating on its surface.

I started up the path back toward the grassy field. The path was full of leaves and twigs.

I marched up the path, expecting to see the lights from the poles around the field.

No lights.

I walked farther up the pathway, shoes squishing, and squinted out into the moonlit field. Harsh the Hypnotist's stage and tent were gone. *What the . . . ?*

I followed the path all the way around the field until I reached the pine trees that had separated the field from the pirate ship ride. I looked to my left, trying to find the midway walk. It wasn't there. Then, as I walked around the trees, I froze.

The pirate ship was gone. The merry-go-round too . . . and the Cyclone.

The Hall of Mirrors, the bumper boats, the Big Tent, the livestock pavilion—gone.

I took a few steps forward and realized I wasn't on a walkway. I was standing on pine needles and twigs and leaves.

I peered into the open space where the park had been.

The bright moonlight showed that nothing remained.

Wait. One thing . . .

I squinted harder, a few hundred yards ahead and to the left . . . the skeleton of the Ferris wheel.

As I drew near the Ferris wheel, I felt more and more confused. Had it all really happened?

I walked around the remains of the ride and looked up to it as if it had answers for me. Drawing closer, I touched the base of the ride, trying to convince myself that it was real.

"I'm happy Mary's family asked them to leave it here," a voice said behind me.

I spun around, startled.

The wizard sat on a bench some twenty yards away—the same bench Henry and I had sat on earlier. A small boy sat next to him, playing with a bunch of toys.

Todd.

I stood for several moments, frozen in astonishment.

The wizard looked at me patiently; Todd didn't seem to notice me.

"What . . . happened . . . ? Where'd every—" I couldn't even speak a coherent sentence.

The wizard smiled at me. "It's hard to believe it all happened, isn't it?"

I nodded.

"Strike three," the wizard said, grinning. "Time to go home." He stood up, patted Todd on the head, and stepped toward me. "Do you still have those two envelopes?"

"Y-yes," I stammered.

"Can I see them?"

I pulled the two envelopes from my back pocket. They were still wet from wading through the tunnel.

The wizard smiled at the sight of them. "And which one is Mary's?"

"The one with the blood on—" I looked at Todd, sitting behind the wizard on the bench, and stopped myself. Then I looked at the envelopes and noticed that most of the bloodstains on Mary's envelope had been washed off.

"This one," I said, and handed him her envelope.

The wizard took the envelope and turned it over and over in his hands. "Ahh, to think that this envelope led to so much. To you coming here. To Henry's last lesson. To us discovering Meg as the mistake in the miracle of the park. So much because of one envelope."

I couldn't take my eyes off the envelope as he continued to examine it. Finally, I asked with exhaustion, "What's in there? What's in the envelope?"

The wizard looked around the park, then back to me. "Just two very, very magical tickets. One is for you. One is for someone else."

"One is for someone else," I said to myself, remembering what Henry had told me. "Is that the invitation ticket?"

The wizard smiled. "That's right. It's a ticket for you to give to someone else you care about, so that they can gain admittance to the park. It's an invitation ticket for them to experience something similar to what you experienced."

"And the other ticket?" I asked.

"The other is for you. It's also a ticket to gain admittance to a particular kind of experience. It's a special ticket, however, that, if you believe in it, will admit you into a whole other level of life experience. It's a ticket to unlimited possibilities. It's a ticket to a wonderful world you never even knew existed. It is a ticket that can be redeemed every single day of your life. It's a ticket, I believe, that we were all granted the day we were born."

"What does the ticket say?" I asked.

The wizard nodded at the envelope in my hand. "Why don't you open it and find out?"

"Really?"

"Yes. Open it," he said.

I looked at the envelope and felt an odd mixture of relief and excitement stir in my blood. I opened the envelope, pulled out one of the tickets, and read it. It was the invitation ticket.

"Your job is to be a miracle starter," the wizard said. "Give that invitation to someone you care about, okay?"

"I will," I said, and placed it back inside the envelope. Then I pulled out the other ticket. The golden ticket. I read the words on the ticket and then reread them. All the events of my experience flashed through my mind at a blinding pace: walking into the park; Betty and the contract; the Truth Booth; the wizard's speech; the Ferris wheel; my life's themes; the screaming carnies; Harsh the Hypnotist; Gus and the elephants; Willy and the shields and swords; the merry-go-round of happy memories; the Hall of Mirrors; Henry's ranching story; the bumper boats; Crank and the Cyclone; Meg and the crystal ball; the tightrope; Larry the Lion Tamer; Strong Man Mike; Henry's final lesson; the Tunnel of Love.

I glanced up at the wizard, feeling an indefinable sense of awe.

"It's your pass," he said. "Your pass to possibility. I hope you use it."

I looked at the golden ticket once more and slipped it carefully back in the envelope.

"Now," the wizard said, handing me Mary's envelope, "what should we do with this?"

I held her envelope and turned it over in my hands as the wizard had done. I shook my head and snapped it in my hand. "I don't know."

Todd looked up suddenly. He stared at the wizard's backside as if trying to figure out what had made the snapping sound. Then he slid off the park bench and walked around the wizard. Seeing the envelope in my hands, he asked, "What's that?"

I stared at him in surprise. "It's, uh . . . it's just an envelope, Todd."

Todd looked at it and frowned. "How come you have it? Isn't that Mary's present?" He glanced at the wizard and pouted. "That's Mary's present! I gave it to her!"

My mouth fell open, and I looked to the wizard for help. He just looked back at me as if I should say something to Todd.

Before I could even think of anything, Todd snatched the envelope from my hands. "How come you have this? How come Mary didn't open her present? Didn't she like it?"

I looked to the wizard, horrified that I might say the wrong thing.

"Tell him the truth," the wizard whispered.

I stared at him as if to say, *Are you serious?*

He nodded and motioned for me to go ahead and talk to Todd.

Todd was clearly upset. "Todd," I said, "I'm sure Mary liked your present. She just . . . didn't have a chance to open it."

"Why not?" he asked.

"Because, well . . ." I glanced back to the wizard for guidance.

"The truth," he whispered.

I shook my head. "Well, Todd, your sister Mary didn't get to open the envelope because . . . well, she had an accident and . . . she had to go to the hospital."

Todd looked up, confused. "How come she didn't open it after the hospital?"

I felt my heart breaking. "Because, Todd, your . . . your sister never left the hospital."

He stared at me, even more confused. "Yes, she did," he said, pointing. "She's right over there."

I returned his look of confusion, then looked to where he was pointing.

In the bright moonlight I saw the flagpole, six dilapidated ticket booths, and the entrance archway to the park. I didn't see anything else.

I cast a skeptical glance back to the wizard.

"Look farther," he said.

Turning, I looked out past the entrance archway. There was my truck, still parked out in the field. Then I saw Jim and Linda's van parked next to it. Then I saw a frail figure standing on crutches next to the passenger side of the van.

I squeezed my eyes shut hard, then opened them again.

It was Mary.

I looked at the wizard; he was grinning. He leaned down to her little brother and said, "Todd, why don't we let him go give Mary back her present?"

Todd looked at the wizard and said, "Okay." Then he turned to me and said, "Just make sure she opens it this time, okay, mister? Promise?"

I nodded, and he handed me the envelope. Then, smiling contentedly, he went back to the bench to play with his toys.

The wizard stood up and grinned at me even bigger. "It's time for you to go. Remember your experiences here. Remember your promises. And remember, you always have a free pass to possibility with that golden ticket. Now go."

I stared back over to Mary, disbelieving my eyes. *It must be another vision.*

"But it's not possible," I said to the wizard. "She was dying in the hospital a few hours ago."

"A few hours can be a long time," the wizard said cryptically, "and miracles have a time of their own." He nodded in Mary's direction and smiled. "Now go to her."

I blinked at him, unable to move or speak.

"Go," he said in a stronger tone. "Make the life you deserve." He touched my shoulder and pushed me toward Mary.

My feet started toward her, but I kept looking back at the wizard. He sat down next to Todd on the bench, and they started to play together.

I looked once more toward Mary and felt myself running. I ran past the flagpole, sped beyond the ticket booths, cleared the entrance archway . . .

Flash. A bright light.

I opened my eyes. Mary hobbled toward me on her crutches. Her right leg was in a white cast.

I walked over to her, half expecting her to vanish as she had before. I stopped just a foot away from her.

The words tumbled unbidden from my mouth. "You're not real. You were dying."

She shook her head and hopped the last step toward me on her crutches. Letting them drop, she looked at me with tears in her eyes. "Yes," she said, "but I didn't die." She fell into my arms and hugged me; her warm tears dripped down my neck.

"You were dying," I repeated, squeezing her tight to convince myself she was really in my arms. I thought for a moment that this was another trick of the park, but I could feel something was different—I was different. I pulled back from her and eyed her cast and crutches. "How long was I gone?"

Mary petted my face. "Forty days, just like I was when I disappeared."

I shook my head. "No—that can't be."

"It's true. That's how I knew to meet you here tonight. When I was recovering in the hospital after you left, Mom told me I had been missing for forty days. I didn't believe it

either. But when you disappeared, I knew it.
So I got better in the hospital, went home,
and waited until tonight to come here. I knew
you'd keep your promise to come to the park,
and the same things would happen to
you . . . as happened to me."

I heaved a sigh of disbelief at it all and
squeezed her even harder. "Honey, I'm so
sorry for everything. I've never told you how
much you mean to me, I . . ."

Mary put a finger to my lips and smiled. "I
know, hon."

"Oh, thank God you're okay," I said, my
voice cracking. "It's all okay. It's all over."

"No, honey," she whispered into my ear,
"it's just begun."

We stood and embraced in the field for what
felt like a blissful eternity.

I finally pulled away from her and remembered my promise. "I have something for
you," I said, and held up her envelope. "It's
from Todd. He wanted you to open it."

Mary's eyes widened and teared up
again. She slowly opened the envelope and
pulled out the golden ticket. She read it and
looked up at me with a smile. "I didn't know
this was in here," she whispered. Then she

reread the ticket and said quietly, "It's *so* true."

She kissed me, and we rocked back and forth together for several more minutes.

Eventually, she pulled away and put the golden ticket back in the envelope. Then she pulled out the other ticket. Looking at it, she said, "I've seen this before. I remember when I got mine—the invitation ticket." She looked over my shoulder toward the park, then back at me. "If I had thought I could open my envelope in the hospital without ruining the miracle, I would have opened it and given you the invitation. I just didn't know if I could. So I gave you the envelope, hoping that would be invitation enough to get you in. I guess you got in okay even without it, huh?"

"Yes, I got in fine." I thought of Henry, realizing I had a lot to explain to her. Before I did, a question popped into my mind. "You got in with the invitation ticket, right? Who gave you yours?"

Mary looked at me hesitantly, then glanced to the ground. "Someone I met a few months ago. Someone who just showed up out of nowhere and said he really cared about me."

I thought about who had come into her life a few months ago, but drew a blank. I couldn't forget, though, that our troubles and arguments had begun to intensify at that time. She had started begging me to change even more adamantly. I suddenly felt an odd pang of jealousy and confusion.

"Who, honey? Who gave you the invitation?"

"Someone who had obviously been here and received an envelope with his own tickets. Someone who found me and said he cared about me . . . and you. Someone who had decided to choose a different life."

Mary glanced back toward her parents' van.

The driver's side door opened. An old man I didn't recognize got out and started walking toward us.

I looked at Mary, and tears welled up in her eyes as he neared.

The man walked up and smiled at Mary, then hesitantly at me.

Then I recognized him.

"Hi, son," he said.

AUTHOR'S NOTE

What secret message do you think is inscribed on the golden ticket? Discover the answer or share your thoughts on www.LifesGoldenTicket.com.

Would you like to live to contribute and become what Henry calls a miracle worker? Then I ask that you volunteer for or financially support nonprofit organizations in your community. I've listed my favorite nonprofits below, each of which is making a dramatic difference in our world by serving our children and our communities. A portion of the proceeds from the sale of this book is donated to these organizations. You can learn more about the organizations on www.LifesGoldenTicket.com or their respective Web sites.

JA Worldwide™ (Junior Achievement) is the world's largest organization dedicated to educating young people about business, economics and entrepreneurship. JA Worldwide provides in-school and after-school programs for students in grades K–12. Today, 139 offices reach approximately four million students in the United States, with more than three million students served by operations in one hundred countries worldwide. For more information, visit www.ja.org.

Kiwanis International is a global organization of volunteers dedicated to changing the world one child and one community at a time. Kiwanis community involvement offerings provide character education and leadership development that lead to life-changing service. Dating back to 1915, the Kiwanis family includes Key Club for high school students and Circle K for university students. Each year the Kiwanis family contributes more than 20 million service hours and $100 million through hundreds of thousands of community service projects. To learn more about how you can get involved, visit www.kiwanis.org.

The **YMCA** builds strong kids, strong families, and strong communities. Our mission is to put Christian principles into practice through programs that build healthy spirit, mind, and body for all. To find a YMCA near you or to learn more about how you can get involved, visit www.YMCA.net.

ACKNOWLEDGMENTS

I am a lucky man. I deeply know that. For the gift of life's golden ticket I first and foremost thank my Creator. I feel blessed to be alive and I can only pray that I continue to earn the second chance He has given me. In my efforts to live passionately, love openly, and serve gratefully, I am most thankful for His love and guidance.

I dedicate this book to my family. Mom and Dad, you have blessed me with unconditional love and you have taught me to be myself and to value family above all. I'm honored to be your son and I hope to bring your love and wisdom into my own family life in the future. David, Bryan, and Helen: I hope I make you as proud of me as I am of you. Each of you has followed your dreams, no matter how hard, no matter how uncertain the future. You have led the way and I thank you for your example and your faith in me. Along with our kind and vibrant grandma, Lucie Lambert, you have inspired me to be a good man. I love you all.

This book is also dedicated to Denise DeVault, a gift in my life comparable only to life itself. Denise, you light my world and I am in awe of the love we share. Thank you for your support, patience, and encouragement throughout it all. I love you, Sunshine.

For the gift of lifelong friendship, I am deeply grateful for Jason Sorenson, Jason Shumaker, Gwenda Houston, Dave Ries, Adam Standiford, Brandon VandeVan, Matt and Mark Hiesterman, Damon Murdo, Ryan and Sue Grepper, Steve Roberts, Jesse Brunner, Andy Breuninger, Erin Kissock, Brian Simonson, Jessica Schwarz, Jeff Buszmann, Dave Smith, Mitch Todd, Jessy Villano, Janine Yaxley, Jean Lange, Nick DeDominic, Dana Fetrow, Selden Frisbee, Phil Bernard, Stephan and Mira Blendstrup, Jenny Owens, and the rest of the SF crew.

Linda Ballew, you are the finest mentor I've ever had and the embodiment of what a good teacher is in school and in life. I am honored to have been your student. You are family to me.

Thank you to my friends and former clients and co-workers at Accenture who coached me, trusted in me, and opened so many doors for me in the early years of my career. Special thanks to those who helped me find time off to write: Jenny Chan, Teresa Babcock, Janet Hoffman, and Mary Bartlett.

This book would not have found its way into so many hands if it were not for Scott Hoffman, my agent, and Roger Freet, my editor. Thank you, Scott, for believing in me, sticking by me, and fighting for me when it counted. You are the ideal agent and friend. To Roger: thank you for sharing the vision, for not seeking to alter the story, and for encouraging me to allow readers to discover their own golden ticket. You are a fine editor and you have strengthened my faith. Special thanks also go to the rest of the dream team at HarperSanFrancisco: Terri Leonard, Lisa Zuniga, and Cindy Buck for your copyediting and production efforts; Claudia Boutote, Laina Adler, and Julie Mitchell for your creativity and collaboration in promoting the book.

To the tens of thousands of students, parents, and educators who have attended my collegiate speeches or my College Success Bootcamp, thank you for the opportunity to make a difference.

I am deeply grateful for the wonderful people at YMCA, Kiwanis International, and Junior Achievement Worldwide who have supported this book. I believe in your missions whole-heartedly and I hope I can inspire others to join your cause. You are truly making our world a better place one child and one community at a time. Thank you for showing the rest of us how we, too, can be miracle workers.

Finally, to those who I am forgetting and to all those who will share this book with their friends and loved ones: I appreciate your support. May the gates to possibility always swing wide open for you.

ABOUT THE AUTHOR

BRENDON BURCHARD was blessed to receive life's golden ticket ten years ago after surviving a car accident in a third-world country. Since then, he has dedicated his life to helping individuals, teams, and organizations create and master change. As a prominent life coach, leadership speaker, and change management consultant, his clients have included Fortune 500 companies, start-ups, nonprofits, universities, and thousands of individuals in seminars across the country. He is also a regular guest on national television and radio programs and an active volunteer for several nonprofit organizations. Brendon donates a portion of the proceeds from the sale of *Life's Golden Ticket* to Kiwanis International, Junior

Achievement, and the YMCA. He lives in northern California but still calls Montana, where he grew up, home. Meet him or learn more about Life's Golden Ticket seminars at www.LifesGoldenTicket.com.